Summer Stars

Kelly McKain

My totally secret journal

by

Lucy Jessica Hartley

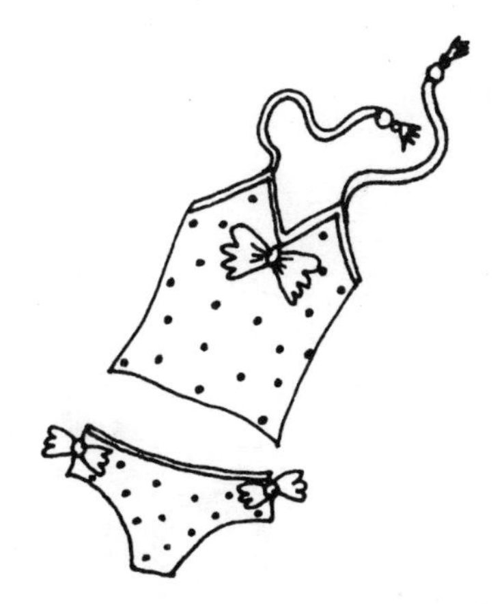

Wednesday the 17th August,
at 6.52 o'clock exactly!

Hi girls! Lucy Jessica Hartley is back! A great big

to my supercool summer holiday journal!

I am starting it now 'cos two completely exciting things are occurring at once. They are:

A) It is my birthday on Friday and I will be 13 – a very actual teenager instead of just a very nearly one. Hang on, let me lean across to look at the clock – it is right now 6.54 p.m., so that's only 29 hours and 6 minutes of being 12!

B) Me and Jules and Tilda are going on holiday together! How totally cool is that?! We are not going completely on our own of course, but with Mum, Alex and also Mr. Van der Zwan, who is coming to help Mum out with the children (not that she *needs* helping out 'cos we are not children – by then we will all be very actually teenagers. He obviously means helping Mum out with my little bro, Alex, who is most *definitely* still a child). Anyway, we are going to Newquay in Cornwall which is known for its surfing – and we have all made a pact to definitely have a go!

I haven't started this journal before, even though it has been the summer holidays for absolute ages, because nothing exciting has happened so far. Mum's been working and me and Alex have been mainly getting looked after by Nan (whoops, I mean Delia – she says being called Nan makes her feel old!). Going round Delia's (you

know, Nan's) house means helping her out with the dresses she makes for ballroom dancers and going to museums and *Places Of Historic Interest*, which is good but not massively thrilling. Sometimes Dad's in charge of us instead, and that usually means going round his and all of us watching *Behind The Music* on MTV while his ginormous pants dry on the radiator and having strange unidentified objects from his leftover takeaways for lunch. Dad lives at Uncle Ken's now because he recently got separated from Mum. Oh, actually, it was almost a year ago. How weird that so much time has gone by, when I can remember it just like it was last week or something. Anyway, you can see why Mum is far more keen for *Nan* to look after us, 'cos of it being more educational.

Of course, being a very very nearly teenager I don't actually *need* looking after – it's all to do with Alex really. If it was just me I could stay at home on my own and start up a business doing makeovers and hairstyles and nails – like in a posh

salon where you give the customers tea and coffee for free and where the mags are not from like 1994 or something but this actual month's. Maybe I should mention that to Mum for next summer. I'll be very nearly fourteen then – wow, that is amazing to imagine!

Me and Jules and Tilda had the idea of all going on holiday together ages ago, when school hadn't even broken up yet. You must know this by now, but just in case you have been away living on a space station or something, Jules and Tilda are my cool BFF (BFF means Best Friends Forever, BTW) (BTW means By The Way, BTW). Anyway, because we are BFF we like to do everything together as a three or it's not as good. I asked Mum about the holiday as soon as we had the idea but at first she said we couldn't afford to go away at all, not even just me, her and Alex. Dad isn't coming 'cos *apparently* holidays are another thing we can't do all together any more. How unfair is that?!

But the GREAT NEWS is that Dad's radio show

has now got lots of listeners (thanks to me, Jules and Tilda – read my journal called *Picture Perfect* for all the rocktastic details!). So anyway, because he is no longer teetering on the brink of being fired, he chipped in half the money for me and Alex, so then Mum said she could just about manage it after all – yay!

When Mum finished talking to Isabella (Jules's mum) and Mr. Van der Zwan (Tilda's dad) she said we could all go, so I instantly rang up Jules and Tilda on their mobiles and we did squealing down the phone together in total excitement! That was about 2 weeks ago and I have been doing a holiday countdown as well as my birthday countdown ever since.

It is especially cool 'cos we are going to be sharing a room, so it'll be like having a sleepover every night. We can have midnight feasts and tell secrets and do spells and stuff. I am definitely taking my Teen Witch Kit with me for max spooky fun!

I have just now been going round the house

making a list of what else to take, which I will stick in here so it doesn't get lost.

To Take

1. Clothes – lots! It would be soooooo awful to get down there and realize I didn't have the exact thing I wanted to wear (quel désastre).
2. Shoes (my special occasion high heels for the evenings, groovy pink sandals with diamanté buckles for the beach and trainers for any boring nature trail-type activities that I might be forced to do).
3. Make-up, mags, more mags, pens for doing the quizzes in mags, cool books to read on the beach.
4. Hair stuff, i.e. hairdryer, back-up hairdryer, twirly tongs, hair straighte

I was just writing that bit when Mum came in the bathroom and looked over my shoulder, going, "Lucy, it's not a hairdressing holiday!"

I went, "Mum, as you know, those are just the absolute bare essentials to survive for one week and BTW, could you not read my private list while reaching for your contact lens solution?"

But now I am actually having the idea to let my hair dry naturally on the beach so it goes a bit wavy and that, 'cos then I will look like a *Surf Dude*. Hang on, what is the female for dude? ~~Dudess~~? ~~Dudette~~? Anyway, the point is I will look cool and Cornwall-ish. Oh, I soooooo can't wait for our holiday!

The end of school was a *bit* like a holiday in itself actually, according to Mr. Cain*. The minute it got hot and sunny everyone went a bit mad. Like, us girls were all giggly and silly for no special reason and the boys kept suddenly throwing themselves on the floor and writhing around, which was meant to be break-dancing.

Obviously Mr. Cain tried to get us to be sensible by saying announcements in assembly like: "Students are reminded that this is a school not a

*Mr. Cain is this stricty teacher who believes in correct uniform and exemplary behaviour at all times – urgh!

holiday camp. Sports cap drinking bottles are not to be used as water pistols. Sunglasses are not to be worn in the classroom as there have been several accidents. Correct summer uniform *only*. Rolled-up skirts, tied-up shirts and flip-flops are not acceptable."

For our correct summer uniform, we have the choice of wearing these gross tent dresses – oh goody, **NOT!** – instead of our skirts and jumpers. They look like this:

I wish we could have a cool summer uniform made of all the things Mr. Cain doesn't want us to wear. Like, **MY** idea of summer uniform would be:

If we all wore *that* Mr. Cain would go absolutely the colour of livid and *Spontaneous Human Combustion* would probably happen, which is where you just suddenly burst into flames for no reason. I know that sounds crazy but it honestly is a real thing and not made-up.

I had to avoid Mr. Cain a bit at the end of term, actually, because people had got inspired by the way I changed my school uniform to make it totally cool for the Charity Fayre and he was a tiny bit annoyed with me (i.e. his feet were boiling in his Sergeant Major boots every time he saw me and he was looking for any tiny excuse to tell me off, like me just quickly mentioning something to Jules in assembly when we were meant to be silent, or having the teeniest weeniest bit of eyeliner on when it is meant to be *No Make-up*, at least for the lower school). So I had to do a lot of crouching down behind the Multi-Cultural Celebration displays in the corridor so he didn't spot me.

Some lunchtimes I was even forced to hang round in the computer room with Simon Driscott, as a way of Mr. Cain not spotting me (that is the last place he would expect to find me – **hee hee!**). SD is a total ~~computer geek~~ – sorry, I mean computer *wizard*. I did in fact used to call him the Prince of Pillockdom, but now I have found out that he is

quite funny and okay, and we are sort of friends, but with no fancying going on whatsoever.

Anyway, to go back to the exciting topic of **MY BIRTHDAY**, which is now in just 28 hours and 35 minutes, I have been doing subtle hints about what I want for the last few days – like writing things on bits of the phone pad:

I Love MAC Make-Up!

What a shame my Moondust Lipgloss is running out (hint!)

Mum is fab!

Also, when Mum came in to check I'd put my light out one night last week I pretended to be talking in my sleep by going, "MAC make-up set…birthday…best present ever…best Mum in world." I even wrote a code on the mirror when it steamed up after I had a bath, saying:

so that it would reappear after Mum had been in for her shower and she would get the hint.

Oh, I am *sooooo* excited. I just can't wait for Exciting Things *A)* and *B)* to happen!

I'm off to sort out my holiday clothes now!

Byeeeeee!!!!!!

Thursday at about 7-ish p.m., lying on my bed writing this.

It's my birthday tomorrow – **YIPPEEEEEEE!**

Only one more evening of being a very-nearly-teenager!

And guess what? No, hang on, actually don't guess 'cos I am just bursting to tell you straight away! The most amazing thing

has happened.

It happened when Tilda and Jules were over at mine today. Dad was in charge of us but round

here, 'cos he was supposed to be mowing the lawn (actually he was mainly doing the crossword and eating endless sandwiches made out of our nice ham from M&S). Anyway, me and my **BFF** were sunbathing in the garden, reading mags and doing the quizzes. Jules was just doing, "What's your beach style?" on Tilda and me from the new *Hey Girls!* (my faviest mag in the world ever!), and when she finished and turned over the page she did a massive scream because of the *Amazing Thing*, which I have stuck in here for you to see.

LOOK!

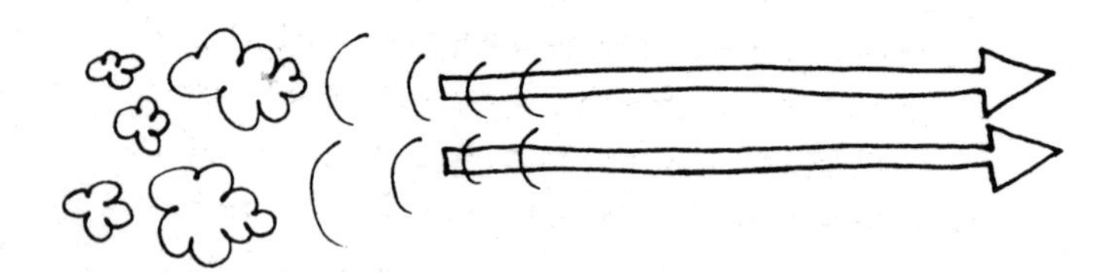

Don't miss the *Hey* **Girls!** Beach Party!

Disco diva Jess Moon will be performing live onstage! We'll also have fab makeovers, cool surfing demos, comps, stalls and games – so make sure you get along to Pentire Beach, Newquay, on Friday 26th August from 2 p.m.!

See you there, girls!

Win! Win! Win! Win! Win! Win! Win! Win!

YOU could dance onstage with Jess Moon! Why not come along early and enter our cool dance comp? Just grab some mates, choreograph an original routine to Jess's new single Deep Soul, and arrive at 11 a.m. to wow us with your moves. The winners will perform live onstage with Jess at the Beach Party. Looking good matters too – so points will also be awarded for styling.

Entry to the Beach Party is free, but please book your places in advance on our website. If you enter the dance competition please ensure that you are available during the Beach Party too! No more than 5 entrants per group for the dance competition.

How totally amazing is that?! We are *soooooo* definitely going to the Beach Party, and also... guess what?!

← *I am leaving time here for you to guess*

Time's up!

Answer: we have decided to enter the dance comp as well!

I instantly rang Mum at work and after she'd told me off for calling about something that was not an emergency (well, to me it was of course, but still!) she said we can enter – *yippeeeeeeee!!!!!!* So tonight Tilda is going to go online and book our places, 'cos our computer is ancient and we do not have the *technologicality* to do surfing of the World Wide Web.

So we are all totally *Skipping Through The Tulips* (which is one of my new phrases I have invented to mean *Over The Moon*). Well, actually Tilda is not skipping through *that* many tulips

'cos she's not sure about being onstage if we win, 'cos of her shyness issues. But me and Jules were massively *massively* keen to do it, so I tried to give Tilda a confidence boost by going, "But you've been onstage with our band the **BFFs** at the school charity concert. Dancing behind Jess Moon with only about 1,000 people watching is probably not that different."

Tilda looked pale then (even more than usual), and she plonked down on the blanket in a fainty way. "1,000 people..." she repeated, looking terrified. *Whoops!* Maybe I should have only said 500.

I could tell Jules was about to get in a *dark and stormy* mood with Tilda for not being 100% enthusiastic, 'cos she glared gloweringly at her and went, "This could be my chance to get noticed for my talent! You *have* to do it or it'll look stupid with just us two."

Jules wants to be an actress, and so she thinks if she keeps performing in front of as many people

as possible she will eventually get *discovered* and whisked off to Hollywood to become a *Bright Young Star*. She has promised us that when she is famous she won't just hang round with Scarlett Johansson and Hilary Duff and co., but will still be **BFF** with us and let us ride in her limousine with blacked-out windows. Hang on, I've just thought that if it has blacked-out windows people won't be able to see who we are. I will have to remember to ask her to get normal windows instead, or at least a sunroof that I can stick my head out of.

So anyway, I really wanted to do the dance comp too, and of course I really *really* wanted to do the costume designing, because my life's

ambition is to be a *Real Actual Fashion Designer*. I could feel a big **BFF** falling-out brewing, like in the way that you can tell when there is going to be a thunderstorm, so I had to do some very quick thinking to *Save The Day*.

Luckily I was suddenly struck by a *Creative Inspiration* about how to keep the peacefulness between us, by using this thing we studied at school called *democracy*. In democracy, everyone over 18 gets a vote and you use your vote to choose the government and that – a bit like when you ring in on Pop Idol but to do with politics. It's also more fair 'cos you only get one vote each, unlike on Pop Idol where I sneakily call up more than once. I explained to them about my idea and added, "That way everyone gets to show their opinion but the most popular choice is the one we do."

Tilda didn't look very keen but she couldn't really argue 'cos like I said it is the only totally fair way of doing things. So I went, "Hands up who

thinks we should go in for the comp?" and me and Jules put our hands up. Then I said, "And hands up who doesn't?" Tilda put her hand up, but she looked really annoyed.

"So we're entering," I said.

Tilda still didn't look exactly overjoyed, but she shrugged and said, "Well, okay, seeing as it really matters to you two. But if I panic and run offstage or throw up on you from nerves you only have yourselves to blame."

"That's okay, I don't mind blaming ourselves if that happens," Jules said cheerfully.

So that was cool and Jules was happy again and so I got some Fabs out of the freezer and while we were eating them we started discussing ideas. I thought of doing a Mermaid theme, 'cos of the Beach Party being in Cornwall, but Jules said we wouldn't be able to dance in tails very easily and she is 100% right. So we had a long think and tried to come up with something else while eating the Fabs.

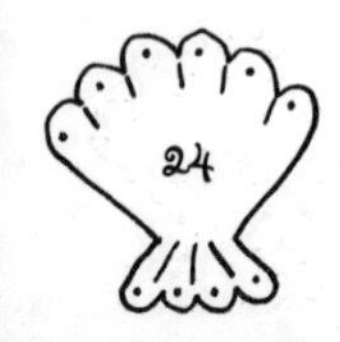

Eventually Tilda said, "I know, we could be nuns, with really long skirts and wimples!"

I went, "I don't know what wimples are but good thinking. We could even wear those headdress things they have and then whip off the nun stuff to reveal cool hairstyles and little miniskirts and—"

"No, I mean we should be nuns who keep all their things ON, like in *The Sound of Music*," said Tilda. "We can carry suitcases and click our heels in the air and everything. It'll be great!"

But me and Jules were not convinced. We weren't keen on Tilda's other ideas of bear costumes or a masked ball theme, either. Of course, she is only suggesting that stuff so she will be all covered up onstage, 'cos of being shy – but like I said, I reckon she'll soon get over that.

So then I started thinking of different beachy things we could do apart from Mermaids and I was struck by another *Creative Inspiration*. That one struck me so hard that I leaped up and shouted, "I know, we could be Hula Girls! It's beachy and plus, very cool and colourful!"

Tilda went even paler than the palest of pale at that. "What, you mean, in bikini tops and grass skirts?" she croaked.

"Yes, exactly! How amazing will that be? All in favour of being Hula Girls for the dance comp raise your hands," I said quickly. And mine and Jules's hands shot up.

Tilda didn't even bother raising hers when I did the "All against being Hula Girls" part and she

just said, "Well, I will try the costume on, but if I'm not comfortable wearing it onstage then I won't, okay?" That is the fab thing about Tilda – even if she's not sure about something she'll always give it a chance. So we all started talking about what colour bikini tops we could make and how we could quite easily do some of those ruffly flower garland type things that Hula Girls have by using crêpe paper.

We also decided that Jules will be mainly in charge of the dance moves 'cos they have MTV on Sky at their house, so she has seen a lot of R&B girls doing that *Shake Your Booty*-type stuff. Me and Tilda are also going to throw our ideas for the dance routine into the bag? Bucket? Hat?

What <u>do</u> you throw ideas into?

I am in charge of the costumes and styling, and Tilda is just in charge of trying not to be shy about wearing the Hula Girl costume.

So anyway, they both went home at teatime and since then I have been working on some costume designs.

Here's what I've got so far:

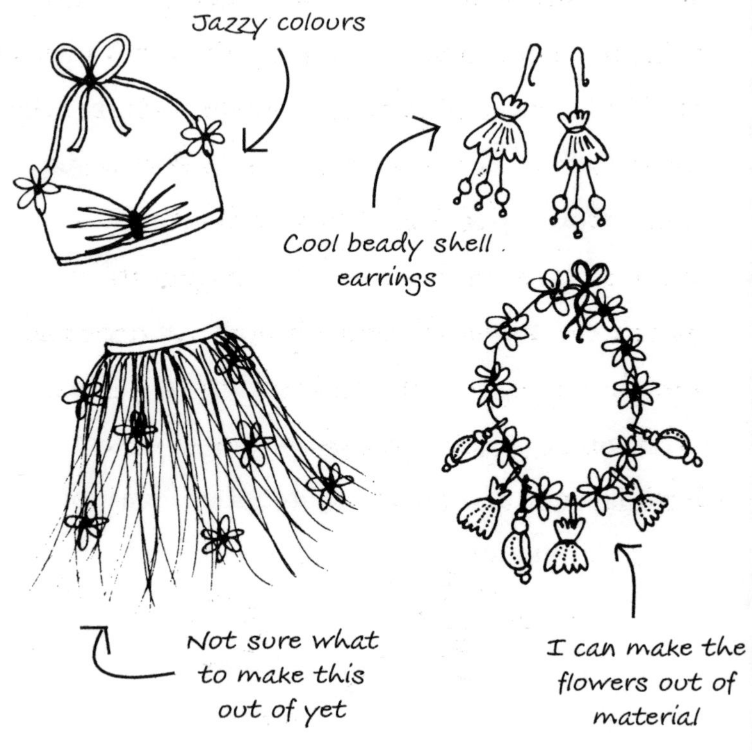

Nan is coming for my birthday tomorrow, so I am right now going to ring and tell her about the dance comp and ask her for any bits and pieces of

material that might be useful as she always has stuff.

It is exactly 7.42 p.m. and I have still got – hang on, just working it out – 4 hours and 18 mins of only being a very-nearly-teenager. I am going to spend some of it pulling the legs and arms off Alex's Action Man and put them back into the wrong holes. That really *really* annoys him for some reason (hee hee). I have to do it now 'cos at midnight when I become a teenager, my matureness might all suddenly arrive at once and I might not want to do stuff like that any more.

Then I am going to bed early so that my birthday comes sooner!

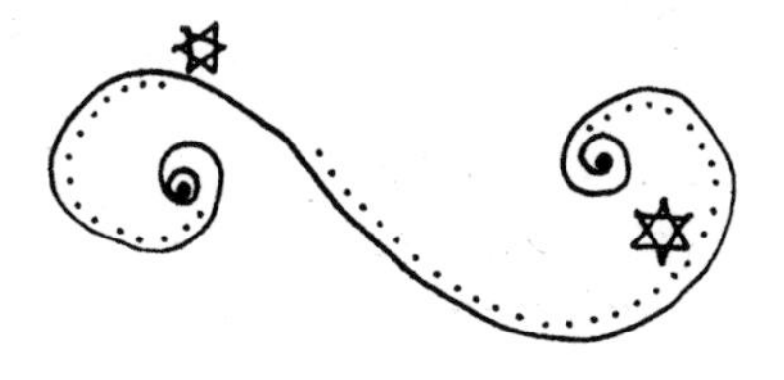

Friday the 19th of August (just!)

12.01 a.m.

I am THIRTEEN – yay!

Now I am THIRTEEN Mum might let me do more things, like for example stay up later: i.e. now it is 12.03 but I am wide awak

Still Friday the 19th of August

My THIRTEENTH birthday – yippeeeeeeee!!!!!!!

Sorry I fell asleep last night writing in here! Just now over breakfast I opened my cards (which mostly have 13 on the front in massive numbers – yay!) and Mum gave me my present from her, which was not a MAC make-up set but New Look

vouchers to go and choose some cool beach stuff for our holiday. I was only disappointed about the **MAC** set for about one second 'cos it will be so fun going shopping in town with Jules and Tilda to spend them! She also gave me a sparkly necklace with *Teen Angel* written on it in diamantés. She says it's so that everyone will know I am 13 *at least*. How fab is that?! I'm lucky my mum is so cool, 'cos some mums would get you stuff like an *Embroider Your Own Tea Cosy Set* or an ornament of a sparrow.

Nice (not!)

Alex also gave me a necklace, made out of fruit pastilles and string – apparently Mum told him it would be nice to make me something himself. I won't be eating it, though, 'cos it looks like he had some trouble getting the fruit pastilles on the string and some bits are all gungy

with his fingerprints in and other bits have some carpet stuck to them – *ew*! Still, it's the thought that counts. I gave him an especially big hug of thanks because I felt guilty for going into his room yesterday and pinching ~~1~~ ~~2~~ okay, okay, quite a few of the fruit pastilles out of the pack when they were actually all going to be for me in the end.

I am off to meet Tilda and Jules in town now. How cool that I have my vouchers to spend! We are all going to New Look to buy some fab beachwear and accessories, and I am the style adviser so we can be the grooviest babes on the beach!

Gotta go and get dressed now, 'cos it would not be very stylish to turn up in my nightie.

Byeeeee!

3.29 p.m.,
back from our
cool shopping trip!

I'm in my room with my cool new stuff spread out around me. Going to New Look was so much fun! Jules and Tilda had some money to spend too, so we had a really good look round and picked out loads of stuff to try on. We kept going in and out of the changing rooms getting stuff for each other in different colours and sizes, and every time we tried something different we came out to show each other. The other two had to poke their heads round the curtain if they were not entirely dressed and it looked like heads floating in space. It was so funny and we got *the sillies* as Mum calls it, which is like the giggles but more hysterical and we just could **NOT** stop laughing.

When we finally calmed down and had tried everything on and decided what to get (Tilda did

the maths so I wouldn't go over my limit of vouchers and get embarrassed at the till), we came out and tried on some jewellery. I put the hanger round my neck with the vest tops still on so that I could see the jewellery against the stuff I had chosen.

Jules found that funny and then we all did and suddenly we were *in fits* as Nan calls it and we had to make ourselves go to separate bits of the shop to

calm down before we could pay, and even then we still kept bursting out laughing and the shop lady must have thought we were v. v. weird!

Dad and Nan are coming round for my birthday tea, so Mum has just been madly tidying and me, Tilda and Jules have been helping her. I know what you are thinking, which is, "Lucy Jessica Hartley, why are you not having a ginormous birthday bash with vol-au-vents and fruit juice cocktails with umbrellas in and cool music??"

Well, I did actually think of having a big party for becoming 13 like the one me and Jules put on for Tilda, but as it's not school time it would be tricky to organize 'cos of not having hardly anyone's phone numbers to invite them. Plus, lots of people are away on holiday (like we will be tomorrow – *yippeeeeee!!!*) so it wouldn't be that much fun with only a few people there.

The mini party is at 4-ish and at the moment we are just hanging out upstairs. I am writing this

(like, duh, obviously!), Jules is experimenting with black eyeliner in the bathroom, trying to make it go swooshy at the edges, and Tilda is also in there doing her hair in tiny plaits so it looks beachy. After the mini party we are going to come back up here and get changed and then all do a display of the stuff we bought today, 'cos:

A) Dad and Nan will want to see what I bought with Mum's vouchers, and
B) I'm not going down there modelling beachwear on my own!

Oh, gotta go. Jules and Tilda have come back in here and also the doorbell is going BRIIIIIIIIIIINGGGG!

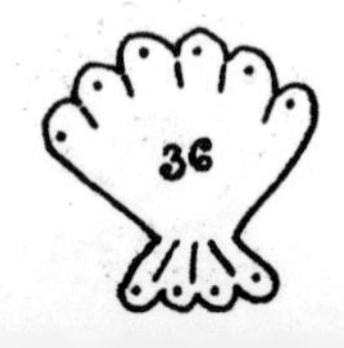

10.21 p.m.
in bed.

Sadly, Mum is **NOT** letting me stay up till midnight now I am 13 – boo! She has given me an extra half an hour till 10 p.m., though, as an experiment (but if I look tired and keep yawning and stuff she's going to put it back to 9.30).

The problem is, even though I went to bed a bit later, after the whirlwind excitement of becoming a very-actual-teenager and the hurricane excitement of having a fab holiday with my **BFFs**, starting tomorrow, I am finding it impossible to actually sleep! So I have put my light back on and now I am going to write in here about the rest of my birthday, so it is recorded for all of time. I am also eating the fruit pastilles necklace from Alex after all, 'cos there are no other sweets in my room. It's quite nice as long as you pick the bits of fluff off first.

The birthday tea was really cool, and we had all my fave things, like Wagon Wheels and Cheesy Wotsits and grapes, and Jules's fave cheese sandwiches and Tilda's fave bacon crisps, which she's not allowed at home 'cos her dad is quite stricty about nutritional healthiness. Oh, I've just thought, I hope he won't be too stricty on the holiday! It would be so uncool if we couldn't all three have the same stuff to eat and Tilda felt left out.

For my present, Nan got me a jewellery-making set, with all these little diamantés and special tongs for twisting the wire and a book of all the different stuff you can create – it was so cool and I gave her a massivo hug and said thank you loads of times.

She also remembered to bring some odd bits and bobs for our dance comp costumes, so that was fab. She brought this amazing pink and orange fabric we can use for the bikini tops. I'm not taking my sewing machine on holiday, obviously, so

she's drawn out for me how to make simple string bikinis that we can sew by hand while we're on the beach. She's even cut out the bits of material and I've only got to put them all together.

Dad got me some HMV vouchers, which is fabbity fab 'cos then I can choose some music by one of the bands I like listening to on the radio, or maybe even get a DVD. So we can have another shopping trip to town when I get back from holiday – *yippeeee!!* When Dad came round he was wearing these sk8er shorts, and he had his pants on display. I know you are *supposed* to show your pants with those shorts, but it is *yurgh* on Dad because:

A) he is too old, and

B) no one really wants to see their dad's pants anyway, do they? Especially not in the public of their birthday tea! Just because all the listeners to his radio show are students, I reckon he thinks he is one too!

I am a bit sad actually that Dad is not coming on holiday with us. That is because:

A) it's the only time it's okay to show your pants (well, swimming trunks) so he would actually look normal for a change, and

B) it's the first holiday we have been on since Mum and Dad split up and it will be very strange not having him there.

Actually, maybe that's why Mum is letting Jules come and we are joining up with Tilda and Mr. Van der Zwan. Maybe if it was just the three of us (i.e. Mum, me and Alex) it would be too obvious that we were missing someone and we would be v. sad. Maybe Mum feels sad about it too – I would ask her but it is sometimes hard to talk to her about Dad stuff. I'm not sure why, but it just is.

While Dad was outside sorting out the shed (which is really code for Getting Out Of The House where Nan was giving him *Looks of*

Poison and talking loudly about what a shame it was that he didn't try harder to make it work out with Mum), I went out to him and sorted out the shed as well. Then before I knew it I was mumbling, "Dad, I'm really down that you can't come on holiday with us. I wish you could, even though you are normally a bit embarrassing."

"Erm, thanks, I think!" he said. He was smiling, but sort of in a sad way and he put his arm round me. "I'll get some time off in the autumn half-term," he said then, "and we'll go away, me, you and Alex. Maybe even Spain or somewhere else abroad. How does that sound?"

"Great," I said, trying to look really excited. Of course I would love to go to Spain on a plane (especially 'cos I have only been on one once before, to visit my cousins in America) but it doesn't feel *that* great in actual fact. It's funny, before Mum and Dad split up I would have loved to go away with just Dad, 'cos without Mum there we'd be allowed to eat snacks all the time and no

actual meals, and stay up till whenever we wanted, and persuade Dad into buying us things that Mum would say, *No way, absolutely not* to. But now I just want us all to go together. It is so annoying that Mum is in charge of the Hartleys and not me because I would just say *Dad has to come, so get used to it!*

Anyway, I am in danger of getting into a sad mood by writing down all my feelings about that, so I am not going to think about how Dad is **NOT** coming but more about how Jules and Tilda **ARE** coming. Oh, writing their names has reminded me that I was in the middle of telling you about the birthday tea and what presents I got.

Jules and Tilda gave me this massive box and I was thinking, *Erm, what could possibly be in here?* When I unwrapped it there was a smaller box inside, and then another one and another one and then a bag and then inside that there was a wrapped-up present and inside there was a completely fab make-up set from Boots with

lipglosses and eyeliners and mascara and absolutely everything, in this really cool purple make-up bag, like this:

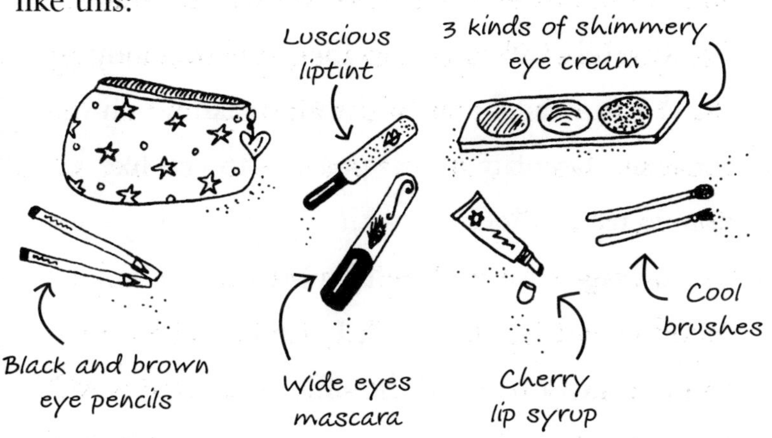

I was completely amazed 'cos it looked really expensive. Jules said they had to put two weeks' worth of their pocket money together to get it and I felt like crying with happiness. Maybe my teenager hormones have arrived and I will be bursting into tears all the time. In fact, maybe the extra emotionality is a sign that I'm getting my Q. (Q means period, BTW. We made that up so we could talk about it even when boys were listening, and P was too obvious so we chose the next

letter!) So anyway, then we had a massive **BFF** hug. Now I can't wait to try out fab looks with my lovely new set on holiday, and we can even use it to do our Hula Girl make-up for the dance comp!

We also had a really scrummy cake which was about as chocolaty as it is possible to get, like double triple chocolate with extra chocolaty choc icing. I said, "Mum, I didn't notice you making this," and she went, "Well, I didn't have time with working extra hours at the office to sort everything out before going away, so my friend Mr. Kipling baked it for me." All the grown-ups and Tilda laughed but even with the matureness of being 13 I didn't know what they were on about. Still, I laughed as well so they wouldn't *know* I didn't know what they were on about – clever, huh? So I blew out all 13 of my candles and made a wish which was so completely secret I can't even write it down in here or it won't come true.

Then we came upstairs and tipped everything from our shopping trip out on the bed and created

our beach looks. After lots of adding things and taking things off and swapping and getting extra stuff out from my drawers we looked like this:

I think Tilda's crochet thing is really cool for walking to the beach and that, but Tilda says she loves it so much she's not taking it off **EVER**, even when we are sunbathing. I was like, "But then you will get a tan in that pattern," and she was like, "Fine by me. Anyway I don't tan so it doesn't matter!" I think maybe she is secretly a bit shy about walking round in just a bikini in public (even if it is a beach), but I didn't mention that in case it was true and she got upset.

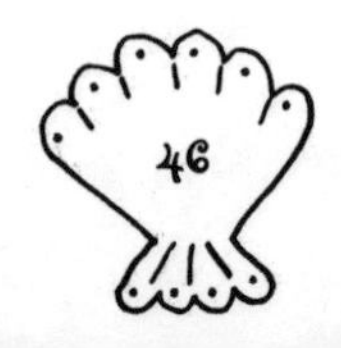

Anyway, we all got *the sillies* again and came down giggling, wrapped in the hugest bath towels we could find. Then we flung them off one by one, going, "da-daaaa!" and doing a model-ish walk (except Tilda who just did a kind of twirl and curtsy, then raced back upstairs). Mum, Dad and Nan did claps for us, and then Mum even brought down the designer cossie that she'd got for less than half price at Clarks Village to show Nan. It is this cool white swimsuit with a really big bit cut out of the back and a buckle thing on it.

For some reason, when Dad saw it his eyes went sort of bulgy and he started going, "You could get terrible sunburn in that thing, Sue. It's almost dangerous. How about wearing a nice big navy blue Speedo instead?"

Mum and Nan looked like they found that really funny for some reason and Mum said, "Thank you for your concern, Brian. Maybe I should just wear a huge kaftan that covers me up from head to toe."

"I'm only thinking of your health, Sue," Dad grumbled. But when he got up to put the kettle on for some coffee, Mum and Nan were doing raised eyebrows about him and trying not to burst out laughing. Weird or what?

What's also quite weird is being 13 – it's not like I expected. I mean, I thought I'd feel like a completely different person straight away and become completely mature overnight but actually at the birthday tea I got a bit annoyed that Alex nabbed the last sausage roll, even though I am not that bothered about them, so maybe it takes time to get matureness, or maybe that is the effect little bros have on you whatever age you are.

Me and Alex still fighting when we are using walking sticks! Although by that time there probably won't be sausage rolls but just Space Capsules or something, but you get what I mean!

Maybe my matureness will only properly blossom when I am with my BFF or exotic strangers. There are no exotic strangers in Sherborne, but maybe there will be some in Cornwall!

Right, I am going to try falling asleep again now, 'cos mentioning Cornwall has reminded me that we are getting up at 7.45 a.m. to go there and if I'm grumpy and tired Mum will probably change my bedtime back immediately, so I'd better get some sleep now.

Goodnight!

Saturday the 20th of August, holiday!

Well, luckily Mr. Van der Zwan has hired one of those people-carrying cars or there's no way we could've fitted in, not with all our stuff as well. It's 9.06 o'clock precisely and we've just set off. I can't wait to get there and see what our room's like! I have got some sweets and mini packets of cereal in my suitcase for having our midnight feasts.

Mum made me take out the big bag of crisps and packets of biscuits, though. She said, "There will be shops in Cornwall, you know, Lucy, it's not the Mongolian desert." And then she made me let Alex put his gross boy stuff in **MY** suitcase to save space *(groan!)*.

Mr. Van der Zwan has asked us to call him by his Christian name, which is in actual fact *Christiaan*.

Yes, it does have two as, that is not me making a mistake!

But it is too weird after all this time of calling him Mr. Van der Zwan to change it now. Every time Mum says *Christiaan* (i.e. "Would you like a glacier mint, *Christiaan*?") it makes me totally laugh and I have to shove my hand in my mouth.

This holiday is going to be just *soooooo* cool!

Still Saturday, but now 9.39 a.m.

We are not there yet.

Apparently Cornwall is quite far.

10.16 a.m.

We are still not there yet. It could be because Mr. V der Z is only going about 42 miles an hour, which explains why my writing is perfectly neat and straight. He even indicates on the motorway, whereas my dad just veers across lanes without warning, usually right in front of trucks. Oh hang on, Tilda wants to do a Style Quiz on me, gotta go.

10.22 a.m.

Well, apparently I am a "Fab Fashionista" according to that quiz, which we knew already.

Honestly, we are going so slow I am not even carsick from doing the quiz back to Tilda! Even Mum is reading *Vogue*, instead of doing what she does when Dad drives, which is gripping the door handle really hard and occasionally doing a *Shriek of Mortal Terror*.

10.54 a.m.

We are still *still* not there yet, although we did just stop in the Little Chef to go to the toilet and Mum got us all a drink because she feels funny about using the *facilities* without buying anything (luckily for us!). Yes, Mum is now saying *facilities* instead of *loos* – probably because Mr. V der Z is quite posh.

11.19 a.m.

Yes, you have guessed it. We are still, still *still* not there yet. We decided to have some music and so

Mr. V der Z put on Radio 3 but got outvoted 4 to 1. The girls (incl. Mum) wanted Virgin FM instead and so it got switched over but Alex complained and said he actually *liked* the classical music, so then I could see Mr. V der Z smiling in the rear-view mirror. Alex is only being a swot 'cos the hire car has satnav, which is this box with a polite lady's voice inside that tells you where to go, like "Turn Left Here", etc. etc., and he wants Mr. V der Z to let him have a go with it.

I tried to hint about the *extreeeeeeeeemely slooooooooooooooow* speed we are going by pretending to be the satnav lady and saying, "Please speed up. At this rate you are approximately 45 and a half hours from your destination." But everyone knew it was me, and unfortunately Mum told me off for being *rude* (when of course I was only being *funny*). *Huh!* Obviously 'cos Mr. V der Z is posh she thinks I have to start being posh too and acting like those Von Trapp girls in *The Sound of Music* who wear

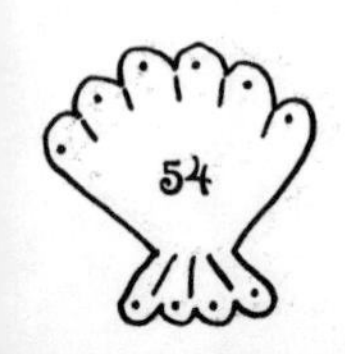

curtain dresses and are almost entirely perfect. So now I am being in a mood with her, even if she hasn't actually noticed because of being in the front seat next to Christiaan.

11.49 a.m.

Oh wow wow wow!

Jess Moon's new song just came on the radio and us three BFFs were all singing along v. v. loudly and grooving around in our seats. We have all gone mega-ly squealy thinking that we will see her live at the Hey Girls! Beach Party and maybe, just a tiny weeny little maybe, we could win the dance comp and get to perform onstage as her backing dancers! Jules says she's already worked out some great moves – I can't wait to get practising! Actually, I'm going to stop writing in here for now and just stare out of the window imagining exactly how cool it would be to win!

12.10 p.m.

I really, really thought we'd be there by now. I have had my imagining about being onstage with Jess Moon, and we have done *I spy*, but it is now boring 'cos we ran out of things straight away after field, car, tree, horse, etc. The last one I did was *something beginning with BPE.*

When Alex finally gave up I told him the answer.

(Answer: *Big Pink Elephant*)

But he reckons just spying it in my imagination isn't fair, or it would be called *I Spy With My Little Imagination*. Anyway, he said it didn't count, and I said it did, so he has plugged into his Walkman and is now not talking to me.

Oh, hang on, Mum says we **ARE** here. *Yay!*

We are finally at The Elms Hotel!

Yessity-yes-yes!

Can't write much 'cos we are going down to explore the nearest beach as soon as everyone is unpacked. But just to quickly tell you that:

1. Me, Jules and Tilda just did bagsies for our beds by running up and diving on them.
2. I have put some posters of Purple Seven and Jess Moon up to make the room less boring.
3. There is this weird china milkmaid ornamental thingie on top of the TV for no reason.
4. In the bathroom there is a spare loo roll with a knitted ballerina tea cosy-type thing on it (but why would you want to keep a loo roll warm?).

5. Everything is flowery – not cool hippy flowery but old lady flowery.
6. Even my duvet.

When Mum came in just now, she saw my posters and went, "Lucy, you're only here for a week!"

I said, "Mum, please can I get a new duvet 'cos the old lady flowers on this one are gross-o-matic."

Mum did her hand on hips, tight lips thing which means she will have *No Nonsense* and said, "I'm not asking you to wear it, Lucy, just sleep under it." So I'm guessing I'll just have to put up with it. But I have draped my sarong over my bed and Jules has put her spare beach towel on hers, so our room is starting to look a bit more groovy at least.

Oh dratification,

there is a black cloud on my happy holiday horizon!

We're down on the beach and I am angling this carefully away from Tilda 'cos I don't want her to see what I am putting or she will most probably be upset.

What I'm putting is that Tilda's dad is wrecking our holiday and it's hardly even started!

What happened was, after we'd all set up camp on the beach and been there for a while and got really hot, Mr. Van der *Call-Me-Christiaan* went down to the beach café for ice creams and Alex the creep went along to help. When they came back they had kiddie lollies for me, Jules and Tilda instead of Cornettos but that is not the *Holiday Disaster*. The holiday disaster is that Mr. V der Z explained that he'd seen a Beach Club up by the car park for children to do children's activities (not

that I'd even know what children's activities *are* because of me being a teenager, but anyway). When he said, "Alex thought it would be fun to go along," I was thinking, *Yay, no little bro tagging round with us all week!* but then he dropped the bombshell of, "so I signed you all up!"

Boo! Boo! And triple boo!

That's when Mum looked worried and said, "How much do I owe you?" and I thought, *Yessity-yes-yes! It will be too expensive and Mum will say we can't go and save us from the Holiday Disaster! If this happens I promise to never ever get in a mood with her again!*

But disaster just struck even more when Mr. V der Z said it was his treat so then we all had to say Thank You Very Much like the *très perfecto* Von Trapp girls and not complain one bit, meaning not even any silent eye-rolling. I knew this 'cos when I started doing it, Mum raised her eyebrow at me so warningly that I had to stop straight away

and do a fake smile instead.

But I know Jules isn't happy either, 'cos when we just now wandered off exploring together as a three, she went, "Thanks for having such an uncool dad, Tilda!" and started grumbling about going to Beach Club. Tilda looked at me like she was expecting me to say, "You are wrong, Jules, it will in fact be mega-ly cool," but I avoided taking sides because that usually leads to a big BFF explosion.

Grrr! and *Argh!* I will have to think of a good plan to get out of Beach Club that doesn't hurt Tilda's feelings or make Mum think I'm being rude to Mr. C V der Z. But not now 'cos I'm going to tuck this journal safely down in the bottom of my beach bag and go in the sea.

22 mins later

This is just a warning in case you didn't know – the sea in England is completely freezing. BRRRRRRRRRRRRR!!!!!!!!!!!!!!!! But it was still loads of fun splashing around.

Alex has made up this rhyme:

The blue sea
Made Lucy
Turn blue, see?

Ha ha! (Not!)

saturday night,

at you would not believe what time!

Just when I got my extra bedtime privileges until 10 p.m., I am in bed not half an hour later but half an hour earlier than I was even when I was 12! Luckily I brought my torch even though Mum said it would be a waste of space. To be exact, she said, "They do have electricity in Cornwall, Lucy."

There is silence in the room 'cos Jules is in a *dark and stormy* with Tilda 'cos she thinks it's Tilda's fault that we are in bed so impossibly early. Actually it's Tilda's *dad's* fault, which I have pointed out to Jules just now, but she is not in the mood for not being in a mood (if you see what I mean), so she has carried on being in one. The last thing she said before *el silencio grande* was, "When we go to Spain, we stay up hanging out in cafés and the square *every night*, and we have dancing and fiestas *all the time*, till about 3 a.m.!"

But 'cos Tilda didn't reply *(v. sensible!)* Jules is not saying anything else.

For tea we had pizzas in town at this funky little place where you could actually see them being made 'cos the kitchen was sort of *in* the restaurant. Then we came back to the hotel and we were just about to go into the conservatory with Mum and look at what games they had when Mr. Van der Zwan did this hand clapping thing like a teacher and went, "Right then, off to bed, children." I stared at him in SHOCKED STUNNEDNESS 'cos it was only about 8.15.

I just could not BELIEVE it.

I tried to catch Tilda's eye but she was busy staring at the floor with her cheeks burning bright red. Then I looked at Jules and she was also looking at the floor, but more like she was trying to burn a hole in it with the power of her eyes and then use the hole to escape down. Then I looked at Mum, thinking surely she will mention that me and Jules go to bed at 10 p.m., but when we

locked eyes, she said, "It would be good for you to have an early night, girls, after all that travelling."

WHAT?????!!!!!!!!!

I was so annoyed but I knew there was no point arguing 'cos I'd only get in trouble for being rude to *Mr. Van der Stricty Dad*, and also poor Tilda was having a gigantic attack of CRINGITIS and me kicking up a fuss would have only made her feel worse. Luckily Jules couldn't really complain to my mum, as it is a well-known fact that you have to be way more polite to other people's parents than you are to your own. So we went upstairs at the same time as Alex and got in our nighties and then we were allowed to read in bed till 9 (big wow, NOT!). Jules was also annoyed with me for being Von Trappish and not arguing. She said, "This better only be for one night, Lucy Jessica Hartley, or this whole holiday is going to be a mind-blowingly boring yawn-fest."

Anyway, I will try to be positive and talk about something good. This afternoon on the beach Jules

showed us the moves she worked out for the dance routine and I can officially tell you that they were totally **FAB**! We got the whole intro and first verse sorted out, and we practised on the wet sand nearest the sea (huh, obviously it is!) so it was easier to balance. My fave bit is where we sort of suddenly whip our heads down towards the floor and then stand up straight again really quickly and then do a hip roll thing to the side (I don't know the name of it or even if there *is* a name for it!). We were all really pleased with the stuff we worked out and even Tilda is excited about the comp now – though she is still mainly hoping we won't in fact win.

Actually, I am feeling a bit tired after all (not that I will ever admit that to Mum!), so I will stop writing now and just lie down and watch the time on my mobie.

Sunday the 21st of August,

the second day of our holiday! Yay! I am in the hotel conservatory having a relax.

Breakfast was cool 'cos we had those fab little mini cereal boxes that Mum says are too expensive to have at home apart from on the occasional weekend. And then we had all the cooked stuff from under these big metal lids, which is great 'cos you don't know what's under each lid till you whip it off.

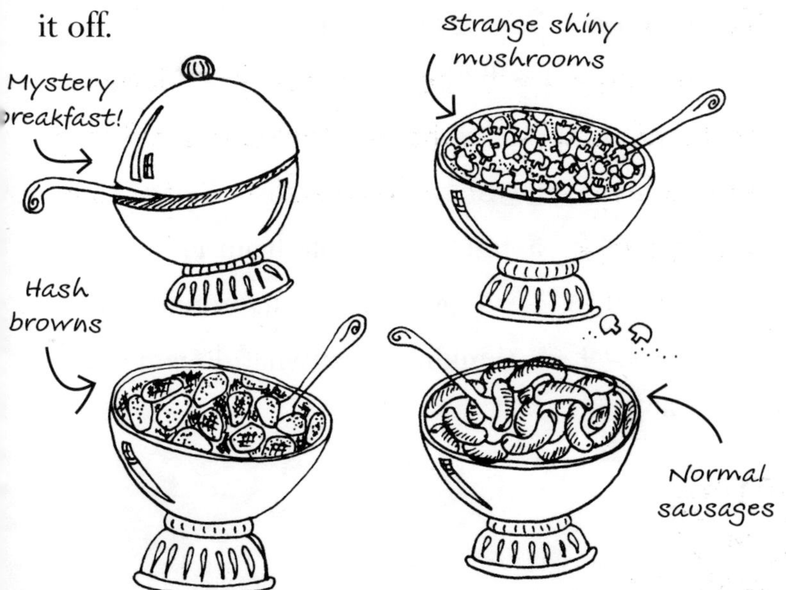

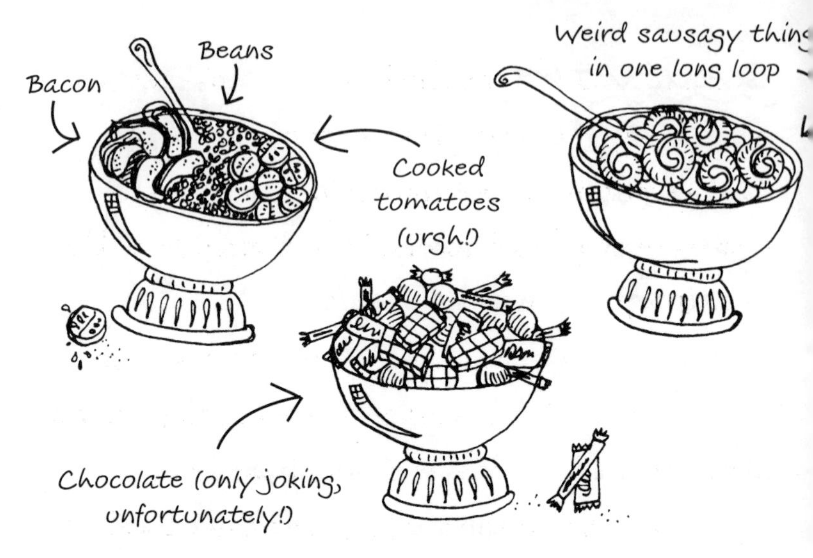

Plus there are about 6 different kinds of eggs that you can ask for specially. I don't know what half of them even are (i.e. *Coddled? Poached? Spanish? Whatsatnow?*). To *egg-ucate* myself I am getting a different one each day and by the end of the holiday I will be an *egg-spert* – **hee hee!**

There is also a big plate of cheese and ham and salami and stuff, which Mum says is called a continental breakfast that people from France and Spain tend to like. How weird to have lunch for breakfast – I am thinking, then what do you have for lunch?

Mum is also very excited but not about the wide selection of eggs. This morning she went, "The great thing about staying in a hotel, Lu, is that there is no washing-up," and poured herself a second cup of tea.

It is a bit rainy-cloudy to go on the beach to actually sunbathe, but earlier on we did all go down for a walk and a look at the sea. Mr. V der Z suggested a day trip to a totally fascinating local church (**NOT!**), and I held my breath, thinking, *Please no*, 'cos we want to work on our routine and start on the costumes – especially as I haven't even *thought* of how to do the skirts yet. Luckily Mum just smiled sweetly and said, "Do you mind if we just have a quiet day today, *Christiaan*, seeing as we've only just arrived." Of course, because Mum said it, and she is a grown-up, that was all perfectly fine, but if I had said that, I would have got told off for being rude – *soooooo* unfair!

So now Mum is reading in the hotel conservatory and I am sitting next to her writing

this. Mr. Van der Zwan is going on a nature trail to spot birds and stuff, and Alex the creep is going with him. He is *sooooo* turning into a mini-me of Mr. Van der Zwan. They both have those jungle shorts where you have to say, “Dr. Livingston, I presume,” for a joke, and yesterday when we went into town to eat, Mr. Van der Zwan bought Alex one of those beige hats like his, too. Alex hasn’t yet got a pair of *Embarrassing sandals* like Mr. V der Z’s, but then, it is only our first proper day here.

I don’t know why I even care but I just wish Alex wouldn’t like Tilda’s dad so much. Anyway, they have just set off so me and Tilda and Jules are right now going up to our room to think about how to do the skirts and carry on with our dance routine – cool or what?!

Now we are actually on the beach – yay!

Well, it is the afternoon and the weather has cheered up a bit so we have gone down to the beach after all (well, us girls and Mum – Alex and Mr. V, the intrepid explorers, are not back yet). Mum is still reading and she has nearly finished her book already. Well, her first book. She has bought loads with her. She says she has 13 years of reading to catch up on, which is crazy 'cos I see her reading mags and recipes and this instructional book called *Raising Teenagers – The Most Rewarding Years* all the time at home.

This morning after the narrow escape from *Local Church Visit Boredom*, we went back up to our room and pushed all the gross flowery beds together to make some space for dancing in. Then we set up Jules's iPod and mini speakers for the music (she'd downloaded the Jess Moon song

specially). It was so much fun practising our routine to actual real music, 'cos obviously we had just been singing it yesterday on the beach. Also Jules has sort of nearly made up the whole bit for the chorus, which has to be really good because you repeat it 3 times. She worked out this part where we walk forwards and back round each other and then do pointing and this wiggling thing while Jess is singing "When I think about you – ooooh, ooooh, ooooh". It is looking really cool so far. She got loads of fab moves from MTV and she also used stuff from her mum and dad's salsa class.

I still haven't had any ideas about how to make the Hula Girl skirts, but I'm not panicking as I spotted a fabric shop in the town, so they will probably have some material I can make them out of.

Tilda and Jules have just now gone to the toilets up by the car park but I have stayed here with Mum. I was a bit worried about her being lonely earlier 'cos we are all busy doing things and

she is just stuck reading on her own. Little things keep reminding me that it is the first holiday we've had without Dad, like when I asked Mum if she had change for the amusements yesterday and she didn't. Dad always has a bag of 50ps ready, and he always gets as excited about the pinball as me and Alex. I know it sounds like a silly little thing, but all the stuff like that adds up and really makes me miss him. I'm finding it mainly okay because with Jules and Tilda and Mr. V der Z here it feels different from normal, but still, I secretly wish Dad would turn up as a surprise and then Mum would have to be polite and just let him join in. I didn't know whether to say anything or not, but things I think tend to have the habit of coming out of my mouth only about 10 seconds later, so I just said, "Mum, do you feel okay being on your own, you know, without Dad here and that?"

Mum looked up really surprisedly from her book and said, "Oh, Lu, you sweetheart! I'm absolutely fine. It's wonderful that Alex can join

in with Christiaan, and that you girls are entertaining yourselves. I'm just going to lie here and read – it's paradise. Now, put some more suncream on. You'll thank me when you're 60."

So I did, for the *Future Benefit* of my skin, and while I was rubbing it in, I was still thinking about Dad stuck on his own alone while we are all on holiday, with only his guitar and ginormous pants for company because even Uncle Ken is away. It's strange how I seem to be the only one who cares about him (Dad, I mean, not Uncle Ken). Obviously I am glad that Mum and *Alex The Mini-Me* are having a good holiday, but it's a bit annoying that they don't seem to be missing Dad AT ALL. It is even possible that he is missing us too, and they probably haven't even *thought* of that! I know, I will buy a postcard and send it to him tomorrow.

Monday

at 9.42 a.m.

In case you are wondering, me and Jules went to bed at 9 p.m. again, 'cos I didn't want to make Tilda upset about us getting more staying-up time (Jules officially gets the same as me on this hol – till 10 p.m. – because Mum is in charge of her). I thought Jules would get moody again but in the end it was quite fun as we got to spend ages giggling and whispering in the dark and telling jokes and stories, before we were even one bit tired.

It is after breakfast and I'm quickly scribbling this before we go to the Beach Club. I haven't quite managed to tell Tilda that I don't really want to go, so I suppose I'll have to Grin And Bear It as Mum says. Mum is going to a spa thing at a posh hotel this morning (not the one we are staying in, obviously!) for a massage and facial and that (so

unfair, wish I could go too!). Mr. Van der Zwan and Alex are going to do another cliff-walking and birdwatching extravaganza (yawn!). It's typical that Alex was the only one who wanted to go to Beach Club, and now he is getting out of it because of doing something educational instead, but us three still have to go. At least me and Jules and Tilda have been trusted to walk down to the Club House together as a three with no adults – maybe Mum is finally getting how completely mature we all are.

Still, I wish we didn't have to go. It will probably be:

1. Full of foetuses, i.e. kids so young they aren't even born yet.
2. Just a room with one wobbly ping-pong table and bats with the grippy stuff peeling off.

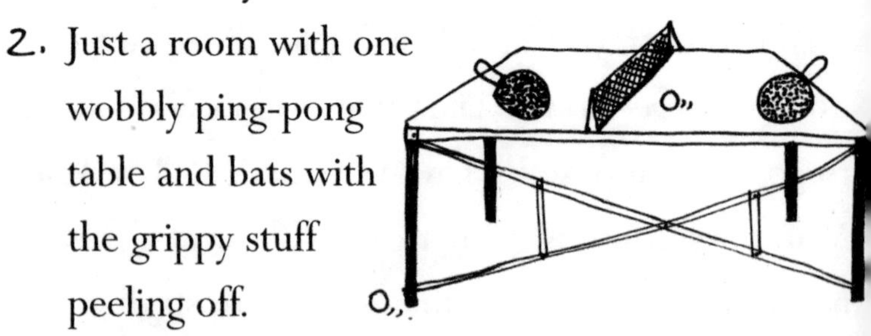

3. Run by overenthusiastic "leaders" wearing dungarees and luminous green T-shirts and doing thumbs up all the time.

We've all just packed our towels and stuff in our bags in case we have time to lie on the beach for a bit afterwards before meeting everyone for lunch. Oh, Tilda is right now saying, "Lucy please stop writing 'cos it's time to go if we don't want to be late."

Erm, you will not guess what I am about to tell you.

Well, me and Jules kind of didn't make it to the Beach Club after all. We sort of decided to go to the beach itself instead, which is where we are now. We can still see the Club House from here, so it isn't exactly like not going at all. I mean, we are where we said we would be – almost. Hey, I know – we can go in a bit, and then it will just be like we're late and not like we didn't go. Anyway, it wasn't my decision to not go. In fact, it was all Jules's fault. When we got here, she suddenly turned round to Tilda and said, "You know, it's not fair for your dad to just decide we have to go to this stupid beach thing. Alex was the only one who wanted to and now he's going on a nature walk instead, so obviously your dad doesn't mind if we

don't go to every session. Maybe we could also just not go to this one and hang out on the beach instead. I mean, what if this is the only sunny day we *get*?"

Tilda looked really upset. "But my dad thinks we're going," she said. "We can't just do something else." She looked at me and I didn't know what to say, and I felt like the cheese in a sandwich, wedged in between her and Jules, so I did a quick bit of staring at the ground.

"Well the only fair way to decide is to vote on it," said Jules.

Tilda glared at her. "Fine, all in favour of going to Beach Club raise your hands," she said crossly. I guess she thought I would put mine up too. Even *I* thought I would. But strangely I didn't. I don't want to upset Tilda and maybe get in trouble with Mum but then I *soooooo* don't want to waste my holiday going to a baby club when I could be hanging out on the beach. And plus, I felt really annoyed that Tilda's dad just decided to sign us up

without even asking us. It's like he's taking over our holiday and worse, Mum is just agreeing with him even though she saw my eye-rolling so she knows I don't actually *want* to go. Of course I couldn't say any of this to Tilda 'cos I didn't want to upset her, but as it went through my mind I found that my hand would not stick up in the air.

"All against?" asked Jules then, and strangely my hand shot up, as if it was hardly even controlled by me – **spooky or what?!**

"Right then, we're not going," said Jules. "Let's get a good spot on the beach and carry on with our dance routine."

Tilda looked really hurt. "But you have to come," she began, "we told my dad…"

"But we *voted*," said Jules. "And there's loads of work to do on the routine and—"

"Fine, don't bother then!" yelled Tilda, suddenly getting really mad. "But I *have* to go," and with that she gave me a *Look of Poison* and stormed off towards the hut thing. My stomach

flipped over and I felt really bad for not going, and I secretly wished I had voted to go. But it was too late and I couldn't leave Jules on her own.

So instead we came down here and set up our towels and that. Then we made up some new dance moves, so we have got a tiny bit further on with our routine, but it isn't the same without Tilda. We got really, really hot but I wouldn't let Jules go in the sea 'cos if one of us drowned while we were not being supervised Mum would go MAD.

Now we are having a rest, and Jules is sunbathing with her iPod on and I am writing this. Jules doesn't even seem to feel a tiny bit guilty about not going to Beach Club, but I do. I mean, what am I going to say when Mum asks how it was? I can't just stand there and lie right into her face, can I? The problem is that Mum expects me to be a perfect Von Trapp-type girl who is always good and always tells her everything, but sometimes I just can't be or I would end up doing

boring *yawn-oramic* things all the time and having no fun whatsoever. But I also feel terrible.

Oh, I don't know what to do!

Gotta go, I've just spotted Tilda coming back. I will be extra nice to her to make up for not going.

still on the beach,

nearly time to go and meet the others for lunch.

Things are officially looking on the sunny side of up! When Tilda got back to us on the beach I was extra nice, like going, "Oh, hi Tilda, I hope you had a good time and also we've missed you so much and making up the dance routine was nowhere near as much fun without you!"

Jules took off her headphones but she was still moody that Tilda didn't *not* go to Beach Club and Tilda was moody that Jules didn't *go*, but eventually they started talking to each other. Jules said, "So what did you do, then?" in a bored voice.

Tilda couldn't help grinning, even though it was obvious she was still **MASSIVELY** annoyed with both of us. "We did actually play a bit of table tennis," she said.

"Ooooooooooh, table tennis, *big wow*," went Jules all moodyishly. "I bet you wished you'd come down to the beach with us!"

Tilda shrugged, going, "Not really. After that we went on a cool treasure hunt in the sand dunes and it was so funny because…"

I can't write down what she said next because I don't in fact remember what it was. That's because I got a bit distracted then 'cos this gorge Surf Dude walked past and so I sort of stopped listening and started staring at him with my jaw dropping instead.

It dropped even more when he saw Tilda and called out, "Hey dude," as he walked by.

"Hi dude," called Tilda, just totally normally, like he was just a regular person she had met and not the most incredibly lush boy I have ever laid actual eyes on.

"Gu?" I cried, sitting bolt upright and rediscovering my vocal chords. I know what people mean now when they say they are *speechless*

With Wonderment. "Who that?" I managed to croak.

Tilda did a smug smile and said, "Oh, that's just someone I met at Beach Club. He was on my treasure hunt team," and then she started flipping through a mag all pretend-casually.

"Name?" I managed to stutter.

"Oh, I don't know. Everyone was just calling each other dude so I didn't actually find it out," she replied, like it wasn't that important!

"Are there, erm, other boys like that at Beach Club?" asked Jules, trying to act like she wasn't that interested.

"Oh, yeah," said Tilda, "and loads of great girls. One's nearly 15. And the leaders are really cool, too."

Me and Jules looked at each other, and my *Psychic Powers Practice* must be really working (I am doing the exercises in my Teen Witch Kit to improve my ~~sixeth~~ ~~sixseth~~ 6th Sense) 'cos I could almost *hear* her thinking:

"There's beach volleyball this afternoon," said Tilda, smiling. Obviously she could read Jules's thoughts too. "We should probably join in, you know, for our health."

"Hmm, I suppose you're right," said Jules slowly. "It's not good to just lie round in the sun all day and we have to keep fit for the dance comp."

"Not that I'm bothered," I began, "but will that Surf Dude be playing, do you think?"

Tilda just shrugged and said, "Maybe."

After a while Jules said, "Seeing as we've decided to come to Beach Club this afternoon, maybe we could just pretend we went this morning? Your dad and Lu's mum will only be angry if we tell them."

I feel like I should tell, but then on the other hand I definitely won't not go to something again when I've said I will – the guilty feeling was just too horribly horrible – so in fact there is no point in telling. Tilda wasn't too keen on not telling either, but in the end we all decided that it was a good idea, for the benefit of our Holiday Harmony.

So anyway, we're not going to get in trouble and I'm just going to forget about the whole thing, starting...**NOW**!

How cool that I might have a chance to see the Surf Dude this afternoon. I'm going to style myself into a Beach Babe in my fabbest new gear to impress him!

Gotta go, we're off to lunch now!

In our room, just about to go out to dinner.

Well, we are off to a restaurant for dinner, but I just had to quickly tell you that the Surf Dude **WAS** playing volleyball this afternoon. *Yippeeeeeeeeee!!!!!!!*

Beach Club really *was* cool, and everyone *was* nice and we were sort of in the middle of the ages instead of being completely the oldest. I found out that the Surf Dude has an actual name, which is Jack! How cool is that?! Jack, Jack, Jack, Jack, Jack. I love writing it!

Anyway, Jack was on my team and I think he sort of noticed me. We didn't actually speak in the conversational way as such, but he smiled at me three times and yelled, "Go Lucy!" twice, so I think that is a good sign, and my stomach flips over every time I think back to it.

When we all met up for lunch Mum was totally glowing from her morning of pampering and the most relaxed I have *ever* seen her, so I definitely didn't want to spoil it by mentioning the not going to Beach Club thing. I was about to say how fab she looked when Mr. Van der Zwan said so first. I felt really annoyed that he was complimenting Mum, and my cheeks went all hot. Even though my mind was thinking *Don't be crazy, Lucy Jessica Hartley, he is not a date-type man but only Tilda's stricty dad with the Embarrassing sandals*, I still had the annoyed feeling right up until our actual food came.

Of course, the dreaded happening happened over lunch and Mum asked how it went at Beach Club. I felt absolutely awful and was about to crack and say we didn't go, when Tilda answered for all of us, saying, "It was good, thanks," and I managed to keep my mouth shut. That is not exactly lying, as Tilda herself did in fact go. It's not my fault if Mum assumes that means we all did, is it? Or

maybe it is for letting her assume that.

Oh dear, sometimes I tie myself up in knots over absolutely nothing!

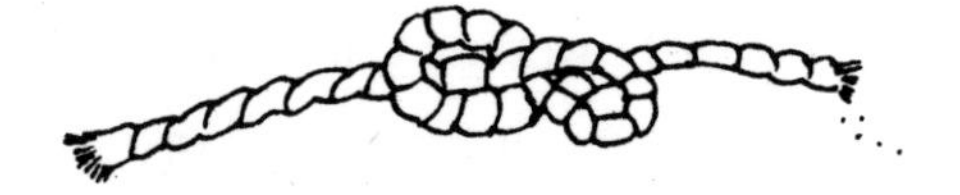

Tuesday the 23rd of August

The rain in Spain falls mainly on Cornwall.

It is raining again and what we had to do this morning was so *yawn-oramic* I will say it quickly so you don't get bored as well. As it was chucking down I helpfully suggested going to the amusements in town and having a look round the shops (I really need to go to that fabric shop to look for skirt material too), but Mr. Van der Zwan (as you can most probably guess) had other ideas. His other ideas were about going to visit the old church he'd wanted to see on Sunday.

Well, Mum had made a different suggestion then, so this time she really had to say yes (although, strangely she didn't seem to be that fed up about it – weird or what?!). So we all set off and because the guidebook said it was a little walk

up a hill to this church we stopped off to get those cagouly things that are completely the *Opposite of Fashion*. I thought only Tilda would have to wear one, but Mr. V offered to buy us all one. I absolutely stared at Mum and said, "You are not seriously going to make me wear *that*, are you?"

I thought she would instantly come to her senses and say, "No of course not, what was I thinking?" but instead she just did eye-rolling at Mr. V der Z and went, "She's only been 13 for a few days and this is what I'm getting!"

And they both laughed. Isn't it annoying when adults call you *she* and talk about you when you are standing right there next to them! And isn't it unfair that they can do eye-rolling but you're not allowed? *Grr!*

So my unfunky fate was sealed, and Jules's too. We tried to undo some of the awfulness by getting a pink one (me) and a yellow one (Jules) while Tilda had orange, which are the colours of our dance comp bikini tops, but it didn't make us feel much better.

I was trying to wear mine in an off-the-shoulder way, but when we got out of the car Mum made us do them up right to the top and put the hoods on and pull the strings tight, so there was just this tiny space to look out of, like this →

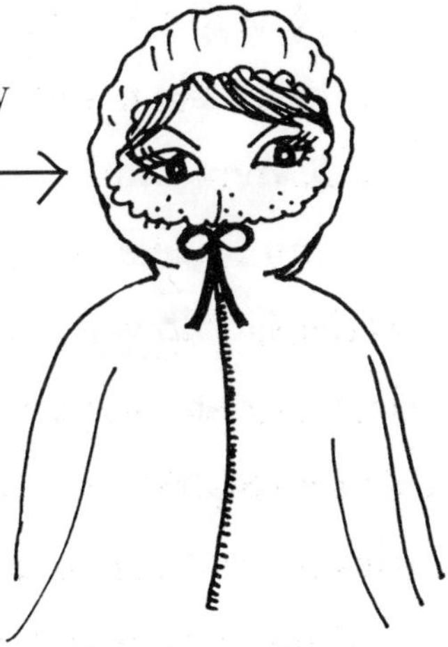

The little walk to get there was in fact a long, *loooooong* vertical walk up the side of a hill clinging onto bits of grass and stuff to pull ourselves up. Of course, when we finally reached the church and walked round inside it I was nearly **DYING OF BOREDOM**, but Alex was asking loads of questions about this fourteenth century rude screen thingie and being completely annoying and a swot. Anyway, they looked round *forever* and I thought we would never get back. But we did, and we even stopped in town to get some lunch in a little café, which was sandwiches and Soup Of The Day.

After lunch we had a walk round the shops (with the cagoule safely stuffed down the bottom of my bag, of course!). There was this cool shop that was like Claire's Accessories except not actually called that and we went in with Mum, while Alex and Mr. V went for a manly stroll around Millets. Us BFF each bought a big Hawaiian flower clip to wear in our hair, as part of our costumes. Then I noticed they had the same flowers on a hair band and I had the idea of using them to decorate our sandals that we're wearing for the dance comp, so they'll look more Hawaiian and also more the same as each other. Mum bought us each one of each kind and I was so happy I forgot to be annoyed with her about the cagoule episode this morning and I gave her a big hug. Jules and Tilda did too, and it was so great thinking, that's *my* mum! She is obviously back to normality after being hypnotized under the spell of Mr. Van der

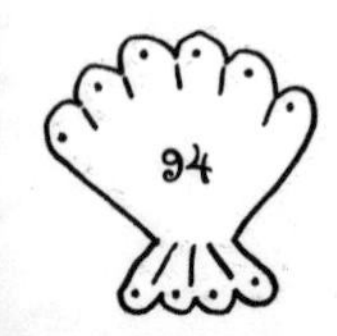

Zwan and his Places of Historical Interest obsession.

We also went in a touristy-type shop and bought postcards, which I have just now written before I started writing in here. I can't stick them in (duh, obviously) but I have drawn outlines to look like them. I chose an especially nice one for Dad 'cos hopefully if he is really missing us a nice sunset beach picture will cheer him up, at least a bit.

STAMP

Dear Dad,
Hello from me! I really miss you and I wish you were here. If you were, Mum would not have needed Mr. Van der Zwan for extra helping out with the ~~children~~ I mean child and three teenagers! You would never make us walk up rainy, windy hills to ancient churches while wearing cagoules. And plus you always have a 50p supply for the pinball and don't keep count of how many Cokes we have. Anyway, wish me luck for the dance comp on Friday – it's going to be soooooo cool! Hope you are missing me too!
Lots of love, Lucy xxx

STAMP

Dear Nan,
Hello! It's me, Lucy! We are having fun (even though Mr. Van der Zwan is really annoying me) 'cos we have found some cool hair clips and some shoe decorations for our costumes. We are sewing the bikini tops you cut out for us together this afternoon and making shell necklaces with the fab jewellery kit you gave me. Then we just have to make some grass skirt-type things, but I have no idea what with at the moment. Maybe we'll find something in town. See you soon!
Love, Lucy xxx

I didn't let Jules see me send a card to Simon Driscott or she might think I fancy him – SO not true!

STAMP

Dear Simon,
Hello from Cornwall, where it is not v. sunny! But it doesn't matter 'cos there is another SD here, like you, but this one stands for Surf Dude. He is soooooo gorge! We have been forced to go to Places of Historical Interest, which you would probably enjoy actually, 'cos of being ~~geeky~~ clever.
From Lucy.

I am not putting "love" obviously 'cos that would be weird as Simon Driscott is an actual BOY!

So I am off now to go and find Tilda and Jules (I think they are playing one of the ancient games from the shelf in the "lounge" downstairs) 'cos we are going to sew up our bikini tops like I just told Nan. You do it like this:

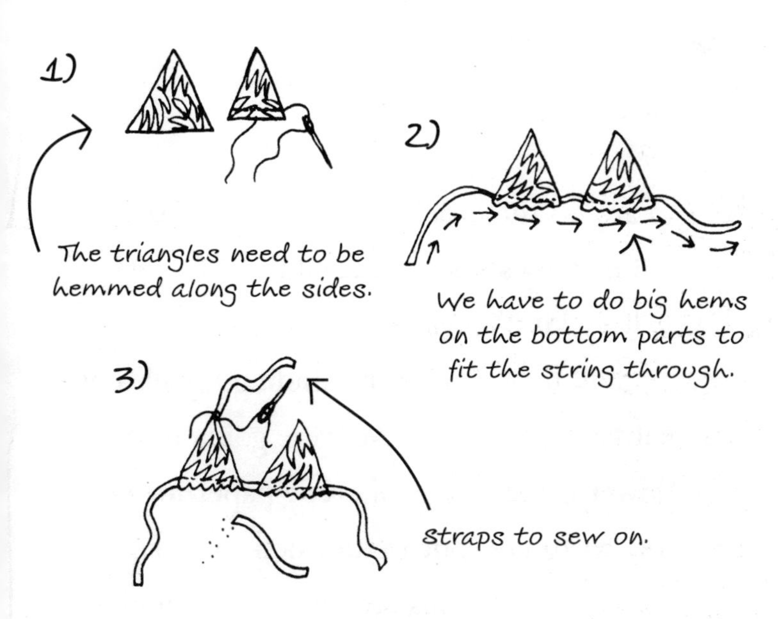

I can't wait to get everything finished and try it all on!

Byeeeeee!!!

Wednesday

It is fabuliciously sunny – yippeeeeeee!!!! Only 2 days till the Hey Girls! Beach Party – double yippeeeeee!

Hi! We are on the beach and me and my **BFF** have just been making some cool shell necklaces with the jewellery kit Nan gave me for my 13th birthday (still have to keep reminding myself I am an actual teenager now!). We were going to do some flower garlands out of crêpe paper for our Hula Girl costumes, but we decided to make these necklaces instead, because the garlands would have swung around more and got in the way when we're dancing. There was also the fact that wearing things made out of crêpe paper might make us look about 5 years old, instead of the 13 we actually are.

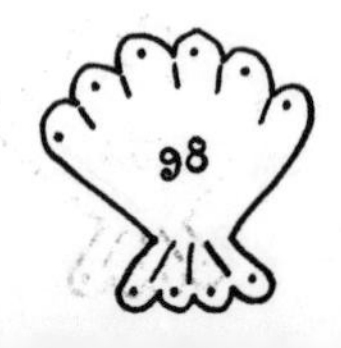

First we went along the beach finding some nice shells (and singing Jess Moon's new song "Deep Soul" as we walked!) and then we had some of the picnic Mum made using just the stuff in her hotel room to save money (she boiled the eggs for the egg mayo sarnies in the kettle – genius, huh?). Me and Mum were joking around and chatting when we had the picnic, and I got this bad feeling in my stomach because I didn't tell her the exact truth about not going to Beach Club the first time. But I just had to try and swallow that feeling down with my orange juice 'cos there is no point bringing it up again 'cos it is Too Late. Hopefully I will forget all about it soon and stop having these pangs of awful-feelingness.

On the good side of things, we had another practice of our routine after breakfast this morning before we left the hotel. It is looking pretty good, and we've made up a cool twirly bit for the end of the chorus. We are repeating the first verse bit for the second verse, but with a few little tiny changes

’cos learning a whole new bit will be too hard and we might end up forgetting it at the comp *(yikes!)*. It’s all looking okay now but we are still getting a bit confused about what way to go round each other before the pointing and wiggling, and we have to sharpen all the moves up a bit more. But I’m not too worried ’cos there are two more days to get it absolutely right. I’m so excited I can hardly wait for the comp!

And we’re going to look fab in these necklaces. We are just now putting them together, like this:

Oh, *eeeekkkk*!! *Surf Dude Alert!* Gotta go!

Still Wednesday,

but now it's, hang on, just checking my phone, 4.23 p.m. and I have unexpectedly just done a beginners' surf lesson!

What happened was, Jack came up to us and I was just trying to rearrange the windbreaks so that they hid Mr. Van der Zwan, who was wearing his *Embarrassing Sandals* and *Even More Embarrassing Shorts* and explorer hat. But unfortunately Mum shot me one of her looks and I had to leave it alone. So by the time Jack got here and said hi I was having a huge attack of *cringitis* about being in the same windbreak as *His Royal Embarrassingness* and could only go "guh".

Jack asked if we were signing up for the Beach Club beginners' surf lesson in half an hour, and luckily I rediscovered my voice and went, "I'd love

to but we've got to practise our dance routine."

He said, "Shame, I'm helping out," and so I said, "Well, you can't come to Cornwall and not try surfing!" but really casually, so that Mum wouldn't notice that I'd changed my mind *specificalistically* because of him.

Alex, Jules and Tilda came too and we went up to the beach shack first of all to get kitted out with short wetsuits and boards.

I can't really remember how you describe all the things we did so I am going to show you in diagrams.

You have probably noticed that we are not in the sea in this one! First we practised lying on our boards and paddling.

still on the sand. standing up on the board is called the pop-up. I was freaking out, but SD Jack promised me we wouldn't have to try that in the actual sea today!

In the sea at last! We had to practise "catching a wave". Maybe it was my imagination, but when we walked out to sea to get ready, I think Jack helped me a bit more than the others.

(Apart from that I was the most rubbish one in the group!)

A wave catching me! That happened lots of times but I also got some cool rides in like this

I wish! That was just my imagination of it.

Actually it was more like

It was quite fun, especially when I started getting the hang of how to stay on the board and not let it go pinging out from under me (which apparently is called torpedoing).

The most fab thing was, I got to talk to Jack afterwards. It went kind of okay, I think. I will write down exactly what he said here and what I said and then I can look for further clues about whether it went okay or not and try to work out if he likes me especially or was just being nice in general.

Jack: You looked pretty sick out there.

Lucy: It's true, I didn't feel too well when I saw that big wave coming up behind me.

Jack: Erm, no, sick as in rad, man.

Lucy (in utter confusion): Oh, erm, yeah.

Jack: Did you eat it?

Lucy (confused, wondering how he could know about me thinking the egg mayonnaise sandwiches might be off): Yeah, but only a few bites.

Jack (looks confused as well): Did you come off your stick?

Lucy: Huh?

Jack: Your *stick*.

Lucy: Double huh?

Then we had nothing else to say 'cos we were both so totally confused and I suddenly felt so embarrassed by his gorgeousness and my bedraggledines that I went, "Later, dude," and hurried off back to our windbreak camp where Jules and Tilda were drying off and tucking into the rest of the picnic. "You shouldn't eat those,

Tilda," I said, pointing to the leftover egg sandwiches, "Jack reckons I looked sick when I was surfing."

Tilda laughed. "But sick means good, Lucy," she explained, as if it was completely obvious to anyone who's not a 100% dim-head.

"Oh," I gasped. "So he was complimenting me! Maybe he *does* like me and I messed it up!"

"Who likes you?" said Mum, looking up from her book (she is on her 3rd now).

"No one!" we all screeched, then burst into giggles. Then we went for a walk along the beach as a three all linking arms so that no grown-ups could hear what we were saying. I was still in **GOBSMACKED FLABBERGASTATION** about Tilda knowing Surf Language, but she explained that she'd looked up surfing on the web and found a section all about it – trust Tilda to do research for going on holiday! I really *really* want to ask Jack to go to the beach café with me for a drink, or just for a walk along the beach or something, but I will

have to learn how to talk Surf Language first so we can understand each other. Luckily Tilda's promised to teach me – how cool is that?!

(Answer: Very sick!)

see, I am learning already!

This holiday rocks!

In my stupid flowery bed, 9.06 p.m. on stupid Wednesday stupid night.

This holiday sucks!

Me and Jules have just come in here and gone straight to bed and poor Tilda was in here already, crying and hiding her head under the pillow. We tried to put our arms round her but she was too upset even for that and said she just wanted to be on her own. So now Jules has fallen asleep and so has Tilda but I am **WIDE AWAKE** and in **TOTAL FURIOSITY**.

I bet you can guess the reason why Tilda was crying – it is Mr. Van der Zwan, who is v. quickly becoming my *Arch Enemy Number 1*, maybe even more than Mr. Cain, the *School Uniform Police*.

We were having dinner in the hotel restaurant, to save going back into town, and everything

started off okay. It is quite smart down there unlike upstairs (for example, the chips are called *pommes frites* and there is no ketchup). We'd all got showered after the beach and dressed up nicely and done our make-up using my fab kit that Tilda and Jules got me for my birthday.

Mum was treating herself to wine, and Mr. Van der Zwan said he would join her in a bottle (not actually *in* a bottle like genies, obviously, but you get what I mean). Us lot were not allowed any of course, plus Mum said no more Coke for me and Jules (Tilda is *never* allowed it anyway), so we all had fizzy water. Mum and Mr. VDZ started doing toasts, like, "Here's to good weather for the rest of our holiday," and clinking their glasses together, and we were all joining in as well. Jules said, "Thanks for bringing me with you and looking after me, Sue," and we all went clink-clink again. Then I said, "And thanks for signing us up to Beach Club, Mr. Van der Zwan. I wasn't sure about it at first but now I realize you were right because

it is so utterly fab." And we all went clink-clink.

Mr. VDZ absolutely beamed then and started talking about how important it is for *children* (meaning us, huh!) to have *Structured Activity* 'cos it promotes both Teamwork and Independence.

When he said that, me, Jules and even Tilda were really trying to hold ourselves back from laughing. As you can guess, the actual reason why I was thanking him for Beach Club is because without it I would never have met Jack! It was so funny how Mr. Van der Zwan didn't realize it was not about Teamwork and Independence but a **BOY**. We were just about managing to control ourselves when Jules did a loud snort of hilarity and had to pretend some fizzy water had gone down the wrong way. That made us all start giggling a little bit and while Mr. VDZ was talking to Alex about karate, Mum leaned over and told us to *Pull Ourselves Together*.

We did all try, honestly, but as you know, once

you get in that kind of mood with your BFF it is almost entirely impossible to return to normality. The final straw happened when we were eating our main dinner, though. Jules casually flattened out her lumpy mashed potato (apparently it is *crushed* potato and it is actually *meant* to be like that) and arranged her ~~peas~~ I mean, *petit pois* on top while she was chatting. Then she really casually turned her plate round to me and it was like:

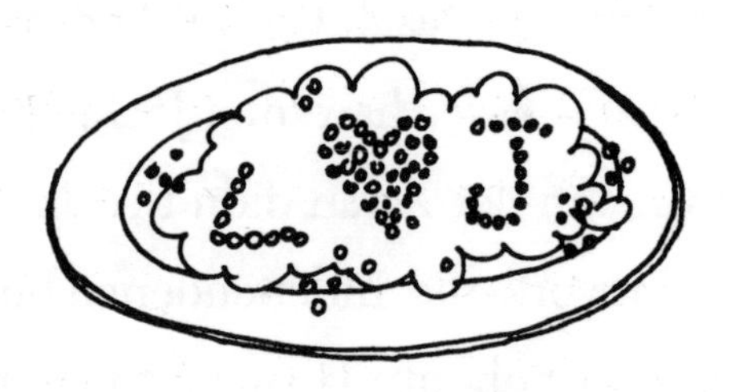

That's when we couldn't hold it in any more and we all burst out in hysterics until I started to think that my sides might actually split. But then the adults turned to look at what was so funny, so I suddenly lunged at Jules's plate with my fork and squiggled out the letters so they couldn't find out that I hearted J.

Mum told me not to be so silly and to leave Jules's dinner alone, and then she did one of her "well really!" faces at Mr. Van der Zwan and they carried on having *Adult Conversation* like we weren't even *there*. We did *try* to eat normally after that but we just kept bursting into giggles and setting each other off.

Mr. Van der Zwan got seriously annoyed and told Tilda to stop it, and she did try her absolute best, biting her lip and looking down at the table and everything. But me and Jules just could **NOT** stop. Alex kept asking what was so funny and Mum went to him, "Just ignore them, they're being silly," which somehow just seemed to make us even worse.

Then I don't know how it happened but things went from being a bit silly to being *deadly serious*. That's 'cos Mr. Van der Zwan absolutely shouted at Tilda, going, "How *dare* you behave like this! Get down immediately and go to your room!"

Tilda blinked at her dad and then straight away burst into tears, leaped up and ran out of the restaurant. We were in STUNNED SILENCE and I didn't even dare to look at Jules. I wanted to go after Tilda but I was glued to the spot. I finally looked up at Mum and croaked, "Shall we go as well?"

"No," she said. "Just finish your dinner sensibly, please."

"It was us as well..." I began, but Mum gave me a sharp look and I got quickly on with eating.

I was amazed she didn't say anything to *Mr. Van der Meanie* about how utterly horrible he was to Tilda. I kept expecting her to, but she was just acting like nothing terrible had happened.

Then I felt like I was going to end up saying something about it to him my actual self, so I quickly said, "Excuse me," and ran to the loos. Mum came after me and pretended not to notice that I was washing my hands with so much furiosity I was almost washing them *off*.

"Enjoying the holiday?" I said all spikily,

expecting her to say a big **NO!** and complain about how mean Mr. Van der Zwan was to Tilda and how we should report him to the Supreme Court of Human Child Rights, but she just said, "It's lovely, thanks, dear," like nothing was wrong.

That's when I found out that I actually felt really annoyed with *her* as well. I can't write down all of what we said 'cos it was loads and loads of annoyed fast half-whispering, so I will do a quick version, just to show you:

Me: I can't believe how he just shouted at Tilda for hardly any reason! She was so upset! Don't you even *care*?

Mum: I agree that it was a little over the top, but you girls were being very silly.

Me: It's not *just* this one time, either. How can you be enjoying yourself with **HIM** bossing us around all the time?

Mum: Like when?

Me: Well, he made us go to that mouldy old church.

Mum: You wouldn't have minded if it was Nan who wanted to go.

Me: Well, he makes Tilda go to bed early.

Mum: Lucy, it's up to him to decide his own daughter's bedtime! Every family is different and you have to respect that.

Me: Well, he enrolled us in Beach Club without asking.

Mum (doing a big sigh): And only tonight you thanked him and said how much you enjoyed it after all.

Me: Yes, but...

The trailing off was me deciding not to mention that I was only joining in with Beach Club to see a BOY and also feeling another massive pang of GUILT about not telling Mum about not going that one time. I hoped I would have forgotten about that by now but I haven't.

Annoyingly, I could see she was right about each thing on its own, but all put together it added up to one big pain in the neck. I was just trying to think of what else Mr. V Der Stricty had done

when she swished off through the door and it was *Conversation Over.*

We were almost silent during the rest of dinner, only saying things like "Please pass the water" and "No more veg for me, thanks". And all the time I could tell Jules was thinking exactly the same as me, which was:

We didn't bother with pudding, as none of us felt like it after that (not even Alex, and believe me that is a miracle). Plus, me and Jules wanted to get down from the table as fast as possible to go and see Tilda.

Mum let us go upstairs and sent Alex to the conservatory to find a book for bed. But she herself stayed there with Mr. Van der Shouty Dad while they finished the wine. In fact, Mum is still downstairs and it's, hang on, erm, 9.32 p.m.

When me and Jules got up here about one hour ago Tilda was already in bed like I mentioned before, and so me and Jules went to bed too and after a while I got my torch out and that's where I started off writing this.

Oh hang on, Tilda has woken up again and she is going to the loo.

I will try and whisper supportivity to her when she comes back.

10.42 p.m.

Well, I am just writing in here to calm my nerves, 'cos when Mum finally comes upstairs I'm going to go and tell her something that might get me in such mega-trouble she might send me back to Sherborne on the train to stay with Nan or something. Jules and Tilda have fallen back asleep so while I'm waiting I will tell you exactly what happened.

Well, when Tilda came back from the loo she got in with me so we could talk. Then Jules woke up (she must have a psychic sense of when she is about to miss important **BFF** stuff!) and she got in the other end of my bed. We were quite squashed up and it was all legs and feet, but we didn't care 'cos we wanted to be all three together.

Tilda said she felt a bit better after some sleep and that her dad didn't really mean to shout, he is just not used to girls being silly. Jules started

grumbling, like going, "Your dad's so horrible, we were only—" but I gave her a quick nudge in the leg to mean *shut up* 'cos I know how nasty it feels when people say bad things about your family, even if you sort of secretly agree with them (i.e. I hate it when Mum says even the slightest bad thing about Dad or the other way around).

Tilda went, "I'm just really sorry my dad is ruining your holiday," and nearly started crying again.

Jules leaned over and we gave her a big BFF hug. "He's not, honestly," I whispered. "I'm sorry we haven't been seeing things from your point of view, and realizing how you felt stuck in the middle. Like, we really should have supported you and gone to Beach Club."

"Yeah, that was my fault mainly," Jules said. "I'm sorry, and also for moaning about the early bedtime. It's not your fault and I shouldn't have blamed you."

"That's okay," whispered Tilda, 'cos she is

really nice and forgiving like that, and we had an even more squeezy hug where I probably nearly broke a rib.

Just then I had a **REVELATION** about something. "I have just now had a **REVELATION** about something," I announced (but quietly). "The **REVELATION** is that Mum was right, everyone's family is different, and being **BFF** means respecting each other's families and how they do stuff. And sorry, Jules, but that's why I have to tell my mum about us not going to Beach Club."

Jules sat bolt upright like she had been struck by lightning and shouted, "What, are you crazy?" and me and Tilda both went "*Shhhhhhh!*" in a panic.

"I've been feeling so awful about it," I whispered, "as if I'm lying to her. I know you wouldn't tell *your* mum, Jules, and that's fine, but I really need to tell mine, or I might carry on feeling this bad about it for, like, **EVER**."

Jules was silent for quite a while, and I started

thinking she was in a massive *dark and stormy* with me. But then she said, "Well, okay, I suppose if we're respecting each other's families and stuff, I will have to respect how you feel."

"If you get a punishment, I'll do it with you," said Tilda, which is massively **BFF**-like when she didn't even do the crime. Me and Jules both said a big thanks to her for being so nice, then I had the idea of doing a *Circle of Friendship* like they do on that **BFF** programme on TV, but we didn't know what to say for the chant.

Tilda came up with "One for all and all for one!" from *The Three Musketeers* and so we did that. I am so lucky to have such fab **BFF**, they are

Oops, sorry about that. I just heard Mum's key next door and it made me jump. Time to go and talk to her *(gulp!)*.

Wish me luck!

Well, it is Thursday at 6.24 a.m.

and things are a bit better now.

I am writing in bed instead of waking up Jules and Tilda, 'cos it is still quite early. I'm making myself stay up and not go back to sleep 'cos I want to tell you what happened with Mum last night before the whole busy day starts and I don't get a chance.

Well, I knocked on the door and Mum let me in and we went onto the balcony so we didn't wake up Alex, who had fallen asleep sprawled on his bed with *The Boy Scout Annual 1982* over his chest.

I took a deep breath and said, "Mum, I've got something to tell you. Promise you won't get angry?"

Mum looked surprised. "I'll do my best," she

said, narrowing her eyes. "What is it?"

So I made myself tell her about me and Jules not actually going to Beach Club *as such*, even though she'd trusted us to walk there on our own. I did say we didn't go in the sea for safety reasons but she was still *really* cross. And I said sorry millions of times and begged her not to take away all my teenage privileges like my extra half an hour of staying-up time.

Luckily Mum didn't give me a terrible punishment like having to wear the knitted ballerina toilet roll cover thingie on my head for the rest of the holiday – **phew!** Instead she said well done for telling the truth, but also that I **MUST NOT** do anything like that again. Like, ever.

So of course I promised, and I really mean it. I feel so much better now that I have told – like, *aaaaaaahhhhhhhh.*

sigh of relief!

Also, she was really cross with Jules for ignoring the rules when she is in charge and has

brought her on holiday, and she wants Jules to apologize too. So I totally promised that I would tell Jules to say sorry as well.

"Is Tilda okay?" Mum asked then.

"Yeah," I said, "but I just don't get why he had to be so horrible. Dad wouldn't have minded. I wish he'd come instead of Mr. Van der Meanie."

"Oh," said Mum, sounding surprised. "Are you missing your dad, sweetheart? I thought, as it's just a week—"

"It's okay, I mean, I do get why it's tricky for us to all go away together," I said quickly, 'cos I didn't want her to get upset. "But it's just another thing that's changed since you two got separated. Couldn't you at least *try* a holiday together, just once, even only for me and Alex?"

Mum pulled me over to sit on her lap, and even though I am a massively mature teenager, I let her. "Lucy, I'm sure you know deep down that's not a realistic idea," she said quietly.

"Well, I wish it *was*," I huffed. "Then we

wouldn't have to go with Mr. Van der Stricty Dad, who also made me wear a cagoule! A CAGOULE! He's so annoying!"

"Lucy, be reasonable," Mum said. "Christiaan felt very bad about shouting at Tilda and he's going to apologize to her first thing in the morning. And don't forget, he works very hard, and he's spending his only week off here with us when he could have taken Tilda away somewhere just the two of them. He knew she wanted to come with you and so he put her wishes first. So he can't be that bad, can he?"

I thought about that for a bit, and I sort of started to see it his way round. "S'pose not," I mumbled.

So I have decided to try and make more of an effort and not moan or do eye-rolling when we have to do yawn-oramic things like seeing old churches or doing massive rainy walks in cagoules. Plus, it will make Tilda happier and that is the main thing.

Oh, gotta go, Jules is waking up and I have to tell her she's got to say sorry to Mum!

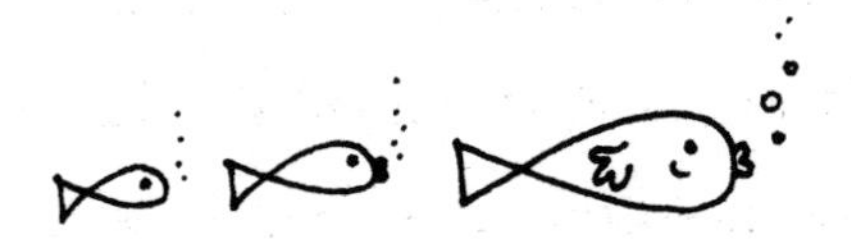

Thursday the 25th of August

Rain again, but we don't mind 'cos we're at the fabulastic aquarium.

We are right now all in the little cinema here having a break from walking round and watching the Informational Fish Video. Well, everyone else is – I am writing this instead (duh, obviously!) 'cos I quickly wanted to tell you the latest news on what's happened. I don't have my journal with me, so I'm using some of Tilda's paper that she brought for making informational notes on the fish (typical Tilda!).

Mr. Van der Zwan did say sorry to Tilda at breakfast and they made up, so she was a lot more cheerful after that. Plus, he said he'd try and see things a bit more from her point of view as well, so I have decided that he is okay after all. Like, this morning he suggested going to see an old tin mine, but when we all wanted to come here instead he agreed to drive us and come as well. We have all been going round together and actually having a cool time (even though we still have to wear the cagoules – yuck!).

When we were looking in this one big fish tank I noticed we could see our reflections really well, and it gave me the good idea of quickly going through our dance routine, 'cos the comp is tomorrow and we need all the last minute practice we can get. Plus I wanted Tilda to do the routine in front of a few people, so she's not so freaked out by the judges and other dancers when we get there.

So we started off, but when we did the flinging your head down and up bit near the beginning with the hip roll, Mr. Van der Zwan's eyes sort of bulged out of his head (I don't know why!) and he started getting annoyed as people were looking at us. But then Mum said, "Oh, Christiaan, they're not doing any harm," and he let us carry on.

We finally got the walking round each other and pointing bit right and everything was much sharper, probably 'cos people were watching and that makes you feel more professionalistic. Tilda looked really good and not shy at all, and she only got confused and put the wrong arm up once.

At the end, the watching people gave us a clap and even Mr. V der Z said how good it was. I'm sooooo excited about tomorrow, oops have run out of room

Later, on the beach.

It is still a bit on and off with the cloud but at least it has stopped raining. The strangest thing has happened, but good strange not bad strange. After the aquarium we went into town 'cos I still needed to go to the fabric shop. But when we got there, it was shut and a note in the window said "closed for holidays".

I had a total freak-out, going, "How could they be on holiday when we have got a total Hula Girl skirt emergency?!?"

"Don't panic," said Mum, "I'm sure one of the other shops will have something you can use."

But when we looked round, there was nothing in any of the surf shacks or the pound shop or the supermarket.

I was getting desperate and saying we should try every shop, like even the shoe shop and Boots and

that. And I was nearly crying 'cos I could not believe we could work so hard on this and then come unstuck like a corn plaster in a swimming pool right at the last minute. But guess who came to the rescue? It was Mr. Van der Zwan! He had the idea that we could cut the cagoules he bought us into strips to make coloured streamery things and then sew them onto another strip to make skirts.

I was absolutely in **FLABBERGASTED GOBSMACKEDNESS** that he would let us chop up the precious cagoules. It's like he has been replaced with someone nice and not stricty. Maybe this is what people mean when they say about seeing another side to someone. I was only seeing the "early bedtime, Places of Historical Interest obsessional, no laughing at the table" side of him and now I am seeing the "taking us to the aquarium and letting us chop up the cagoules" side. How amazing is that?!

We have all been sitting here (even Mum and Alex and Mr. Van der Zwan) in pairs cutting up the

strips and sewing them onto the waistband pieces. Mum is with Jules (who has said sorry about Beach Club, so that's all okay now), and Tilda is with her dad and I am with Alex. For once I am glad we are inside all Mr. Van der Zwan's windbreaks, 'cos otherwise all the strips would blow away. We are now having a break from the cutting and sewing and Jules is having a cheese sandwich from the cool box, but even unfinished the skirts look really good, like this:

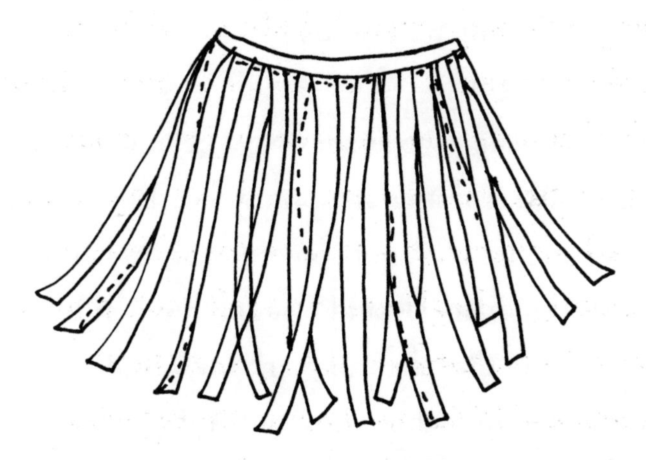

I have also had the idea of adding some sequins from the bag in Nan's jewellery-making kit so that when we twirl around we will look all sparkly.

Back at the hotel

Well, we have now finished all the Hula Girl skirts and when we got back here we stuck the sequins on them. They look really great. We are going to have a *Full Dress Rehearsal* later on when the glue has dried.

We aren't doing the routine again before that in case it gets too stale, but we have each been practising the bits we find hardest over and over to get them right.

My Surf Language lessons have been going well too and Tilda is testing me on my words in a minute. She has even put some pencils in her scrunchy bun hairstyle and found a red pen from somewhere so that she can mark my work! She is obviously missing school. I'm not. I wish this holiday could go on forever, and we could just stay here using shampoo out of tiny little bottles and having *Mystery Breakfast Covers* with unusual

stuff under them, and getting really good at surfing.

Oh, Tilda says the test is ready now. I will stick it in when I have finished.

The Elms Hotel

Surf Language Level One.

Candidate's name: *Lucy Jessica Hartley*

1. Translate the following Surf Language vocabulary into standard English:

Rad = *cool* ✓

Mullering = *falling off your board* ✓

Wipe out = *also falling off your board* ✓

Grommet = *young surfer (e.g. Jack)* ✓

Stick = *your board* ✓

Donut = *erm, scrummy jam-filled cake type thing?* ✗ **Falling off your board**

Sick = *good (strangely)* ✓

Rock = *the same as normal language, as in "you rock", not as in a stone* ✓

The Elms Hotel

Stoked = *happy* ✓

Dude = *cool person* ✓

9 out of 10!

2. Translate the following sentence into Surf Language:

Oh dear, I have fallen off my board, how uncool!

Oh dear, I have mulleringly wiped out. How non-rad!

✓ V.G.

Pass!

Tilda and Jules did whooping and cheering for me when I passed and I took a big bow.

Then we all got silly again and they made me this certificate:

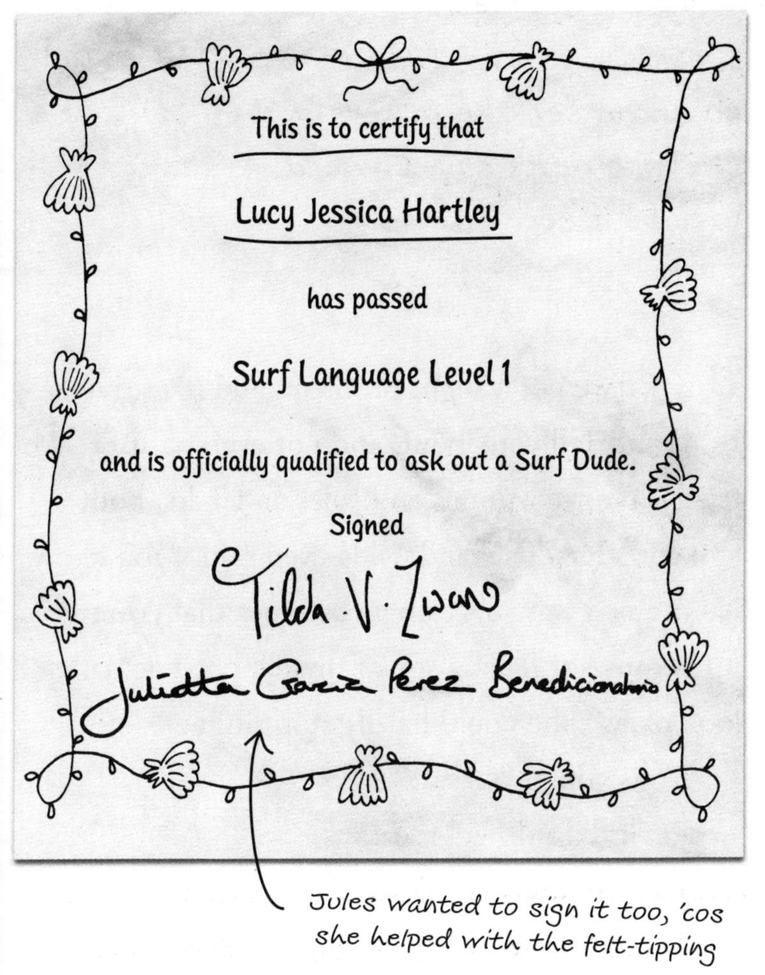
This is to certify that

Lucy Jessica Hartley

has passed

Surf Language Level 1

and is officially qualified to ask out a Surf Dude.

Signed

Tilda V. Zwan

Julietta Garcia Perez Benedicionatorio

Gotta go now as we're trying on our whole dance comp outfits and having a dress rehearsal!

Cool or what?!

Before dinner –

I told Jules and Tilda to go and meet the others in the lobby and say I would just be a sec.

Um. I have got a slight problem, and it's something I can only tell you about, and not even my **BFF**. We tried on our costumes and Jules and Tilda both looked **A-MAZING** and Tilda even said, "You know, it's funny, I was suggesting costumes that covered us up because of feeling shy of myself, but I actually look okay." She could hardly stop smiling.

I was going, "Great!"

But I did not feel great.

You see, my you-know-whats have still not grown hardly one bit, while Jules and Tilda are both getting their *Womanly Curves* as Mum calls it. I just looked like a tiny child next to them and I felt really self-conscious-ish in my bikini top. There is

no way I want to wear it onstage in front of loads of other girls and judges! But I couldn't say anything to Tilda and Jules, 'cos of the Hula Girl costumes being all my idea and also because of it being too late to come up with anything else.

The *Full Dress Rehearsal* went okay, but I felt much more shy in the bikini top and didn't exactly fling myself into the routine as much as normal. Luckily Jules and Tilda were concentrating so hard themselves they didn't exactly notice. But what if me feeling like this and not being confident makes me dance badly tomorrow and maybe even loses the comp for us?

That would be awful – and all because of my annoying lack of you-know-whats!

Oh, what am I going to do?

After tea

(We went back to that fab pizza place – yum!) Locked in the bathroom for maximum secretness.

I have had a totally fab idea about the secret worry I told you about before I had to go out. Jules is right now doing made-up karate with Alex in Mum's room and Tilda is downstairs playing a game with her dad, so I have quickly got time to write my idea down.

Well, I was just standing here trying out Tilda's Brazil Nut Butter Body Moisturizer and staring at the weird knitted ballerina loo-roll-covering doll thing when I was suddenly struck by a *Creative Inspiration*, which is that I could stuff some loo paper in my bikini top to make my you-know-

whats look bigger. I have just tried it out and if I fold it really carefully no one will be able to tell that's what it is. It makes me look really, really cool! If Jules and Tilda notice anything different I'll just tell them I had a growth spurt overnight because of the sun. Phew! So glad I have solved that problem before tomorrow! I just wish my real ones would hurry up and get on with growing!

Oops! That's the bedroom door, gotta go!

Friday the 26th of August,

dance comp and Beach Party day – whoopee!!!!!!

We are setting off for the dance comp soon but before we do I just want to write down in here about how we got ready in all our stuff. I am so excited I could just *Spontaneously Combust.*

Tilda and Jules are mega-excited too and instead of bursting into flames we all keep bursting into squealy hugs together. Our finished costumes look really cool! This is everything we did this morning to get ready:

We painted our fingernails and toenails in the three colours of orange, yellow and pink to match our costumes.

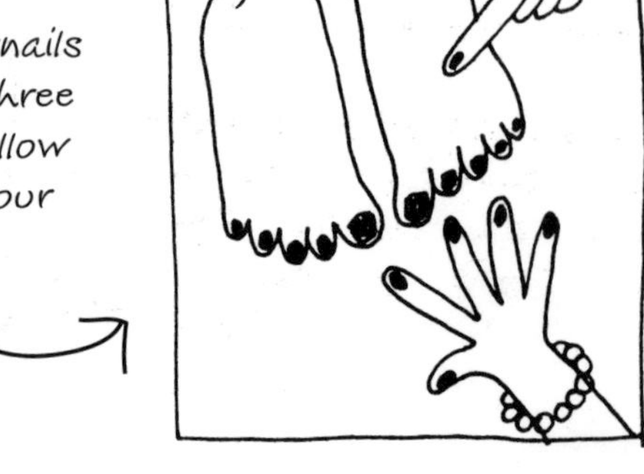

We used my cool birthday present kit to do our make-up all the same as each other.

We did our hair the same too, with the fab clips that we bought from the shop like Claire's.

We got into our costumes.

I secretly added an extra something to mine (shhhh!) but Jules and Tilda didn't seem to notice.

We also just had a last practice and we decided to add the move from the surf lesson to the beginning of our routine, so you get this cool bit where we start off lying on the floor and then we pop up into the surf position and do the dancing. I think that beginning makes it really original and might even win the comp for us.

Gotta go downstairs and get in the car now – *urgh!* I am right now wishing I hadn't had two lots of coddled eggs for breakfast!

At the dance comp!

I can hardly believe we are actually here!

Just quickly writing this before we go on! The stage we're right now sitting on must have been built overnight 'cos it wasn't here yesterday. Mum had to sign me and Jules in, and fill in these forms about whether we are asthmatic or diabetic or anything, and Mr. Van der Zwan did the same for Tilda. Then us three went up to the desk linking arms and handed our forms in to this nice lady called Janie who works for *Hey Girls!* mag and we got given our number, which is 17. Having the number made it feel *Absolutely Completely Real* and we have got even more excited (if that is possible!).

There are three judges sitting in a line behind a table, shuffling our forms, and there are girls milling round everywhere, stretching and stuff, and

some mums. My actual mum has gone on a cliff walk with Alex and Mr. Van der Zwan, though – they did offer to stay but we thought it would just make us more nervous, so they are coming back at 1 p.m. to meet us. We have been trusted to stay exactly here after the dance comp ends, which we definitely will after the Beach Club incident.

There are about 30 sets of girls here and apparently we are only dancing three sets at a time because of space on the stage. Some of the girls here sound Cornwall-ish so they must live here all the time, and we've met some girls from as far away as London or even Up North. It's really interesting to see everyone's costumes, they have all made loads of effort. Most of the groups are just done up like pop stars in denim minis and footless tights and that, and there are some in matching things like these bright pink catsuits, or the same gypsy skirts, and there is one group of princesses and another of punks, but no other Hula Girls – *phew!*

Just to quickly tell you that...

The first round went well (some girls are still dancing now, so we haven't heard if we're through yet). But we remembered it all, and we didn't get mixed up on the walking round each other part. Tilda was quite nervous and it showed a bit, but she did remember to put the right arm up in the chorus so we all matched and I think it was mainly okay. I have to go now because I need to cross all my fingers for getting through, and I can't do that and write at the same time.

We're through to the second round!

Yaaaaaaaaaaaaaaaaaaaaaaaaaaaaa
aaaaaaaaaaaaaaaaaaaaaaaaaaaaa
aaaaaaaaaaaay!!
!!

14 mins later

That second round went better, we were more relaxed and remembered about smiling, and there was a bit more *oomph*! I just hope it's enough to get us through to the final. Okay, have to go and cross everything again, fingers are not enough – we are all going to cross our legs and arms and I will even try crossing my toes.

Guess what?!

We're in the final round!

It is out of three groups, and this time we have to do it one group at a time. We're up against these okayish girls from Truro who I don't know the names of, and also these other girls called Hayley, Tanya and Ranjita. Unfortunately they are

really good. They are also *really* horrible 'cos when it was announced that we were in the last round, Hayley said *really* loudly to her friends, "Don't worry about them, we'll walk it. That blonde girl dances like a robot." Obviously they meant Tilda and she was really upset and I had to do loads of persuading her that they are only trying to put us off so that they win. Tilda also cheered up when Jules told Hayley, "Any more comments like that and I'll deck you till you fall down a manhole!"

So we have had a group hug and decided that we are not going to let them get to us. Nothing is going to stop us from giving this our very best shot. Oh, we're on – wish us luck!

Oh.

Sorry this is on hand towel. The loo paper in this portaloo is v. posh as it's the backstage one Jess Moon uses, and it's all quilty so no good for writing on.

From the fact I have locked myself in here crying and writing on a hand towel with a pen from the cleaning rota I think you can guess that I have not got good news. Well, the thing is, I have had a ginormous attack of CRINGITIS, 'cos I've had the biggest cringe in the whole history of cringes ever!

What happened was, the final round was all going really well, we were at the third chorus right near the end, and we did the double spin thing and suddenly—

Oh I can hardly stand to write this—

Okay I will just scribble it down really quickly with my eyes shut.

The loo paper came unravelling out of my top and was flowing alongside me like a streamer. I was so utterly horrified that I lost my balance and fell over, and everyone was just staring at me.

And then I ran off the stage.

Obviously.

As I ran off, I heard a huge burst of laughter. Now I will have to live in this portaloo forever – what a horrible thought. Still, it is less horrible than having to go out there again and face everyone when they absolutely ALL saw.

I can hear people coming – oh I wish I was small enough to flush myself down the loo and escape!

I just really have to catch you up on what happened!

I am right now on the beach waiting for Mum and Mr. Van der Zwan and Alex to arrive. Jules and Tilda have gone to get us drinks from the little beach café, and I am staying here so that if Mum comes she'll still be able to find us. (See, I really meant it when I promised to go where I was told!) Plus, I have time to quickly write this. I am resisting blurting out everything straight away, and I am going to make myself start from where I left off.

Well, Jules and Tilda psychically knew I would run into the loos and they came straight after me and made me open the door by threatening to tell everyone where I was.

Tilda was all mature, like going, "Lucy, there's no need to be embarrassed – no one cares."

"But they all saw the loo paper coming out of

my bikini top!" I wailed. "And I heard them all laughing at me – so don't try and pretend they weren't!"

Tilda blushed. "Some were. A bit," she admitted. "But so what? You're really confident! You don't normally let little things bother you."

"But Tilda," I wailed. "It was a great big massivo thing – the most *cringy cringitis* attack I've ever had!"

I looked at Jules for supportivity but her face was just *SO dark and stormy* I thought thunder and lightning might start coming out of her eyes or something.

"We've probably lost the competition now, thanks to **YOU**," she snarled. "What on earth were you doing putting loo paper down your top anyway?"

I felt myself nearly start crying then. "I just

wanted to look more like you and Tilda," I gabbled. "You're both getting your Womanly Curves and I still haven't got hardly anything. When we all tried on our costumes I felt really babyish next to you."

Tilda put her arm round me. "Lucy, it doesn't matter. All the girls here are at different stages and ages. Everyone's unique," she said gently. "You look great exactly how you are!"

I realized then that she was right, and I wished I'd never thought of the stupid loo paper idea in the first place, but sadly I couldn't go back in time and change what happened.

"Right, let's go and hear the results," said Jules then. "Not that there's much point. You running off's probably lost it for us anyway!" And she gave me such a horrible look I thought I might just dissolve into a puddle of shame on the ground.

"Oh, I'm *soooooo* sorry that me **DYING** of embarrassment and having to live in a portaloo forever is inconvenient for you," I said sarkily.

"Anyway, it doesn't matter about the results. Even if we did win there's no way I'm ever getting up on that stage with those people who saw what happened all watching me, especially not that horrible Hayley girl!"

"Fine! Ruin my life then!" Jules yelled.

"Why can't you just care about *me* for once?" I yelled back. "I am *traumatized*, in case you hadn't noticed!"

"Calm down, both of you!" yelled Tilda, so loud it made us both jump and shut up. "Lucy, going onstage in front of hundreds of people was my worst nightmare, but I got over it and I'm here and if we win I'm going to go for it. I understand how you feel but you're brave and strong and you can get over this. You still want to dance with Jess Moon, don't you?"

"Well, yes, of course, but there's no way I can get up there, even just to hear the results," I grumbled. "I mean, what will Hayley and that say?"

"Who cares?" said Tilda. "All that matters is that we don't give up, and that we stick together," she added, giving Jules a *Meaningful stare*. "Like we *promised* to 2 nights ago."

Jules sighed. "Sorry I got mad with you, Lu," she mumbled. "I was just thinking of myself 'cos we've got a shot at winning and I really *really* want to do this."

"And we still might!" cried Tilda. "So let's go and find out the results together."

Tilda put her arm round Jules and Jules did it back to her. "One for all and all for one?" asked Tilda.

"Yeah, okay," I half-whispered, although my legs had turned to water. I put my arms round them too and we made a huddle and chanted "*One for all and all for one*". "Except, can we think of a better saying next time?" I asked and they both giggled and gave me an extra squeeze.

So we walked back up to the stage and it was only a few steps across to the judges' table but it

felt like about a mile on my trembly legs. I could hear Hayley sniggering with her lot as we stood there waiting for the judges to come back from conferencing with each other.

Please don't mention it, please don't mention it, pleasy please please, I was thinking over and over in my head.

But then Hayley turned round to me and went, "You stuffed your bra," really loudly. For a moment I was *mortified* (as in so embarrassed that you actually want to drop dead), and then Tilda squeezed my hand and Jules gave Hayley a killer glare and I remembered that I wasn't alone.

"Takes one to know one!" I said, thinking of what Alex would say. Sometimes it is very useful to have an annoying little brother.

"What? That doesn't even make sense!" Hayley mumbled, but she couldn't add anything else because the judges came back.

The main judge, Sarah, who is Jess's choreographer, did a speech about how the

standard was very high, and lovely to see so many of us here, and then she went, "And I am delighted to announce that the winners of the Hey Girls! Beach Party dance competition are..." Then there was this long pause like on X Factor where you nearly pass out from the suspense.

"Lucy, Jules and Tilda," she finished.

I absolutely couldn't believe it! We had won even though I ran off at the end! Of course, Hayley and her friends started whining about how it wasn't fair, but we hardly heard them. The main judge shook hands with us and said she especially loved our costumes and we got extra points for looking so fab and making such an effort with them. That was so cool and I'm sure those few extra points made us win the comp!

Anyway, Jules grabbed me and gave me a massive hug and cried, "Lucy, you haven't completely ruined my life after all!"

Tilda joined in too and we all did jumping up and down and squealing. "This is so great!" she

cried. "Thanks for persuading me to do this! I can't wait to get on that stage now!"

Then we realized that all the other girls were clapping so we all held hands and took a bow. I knew that some of them would most likely go home and tell their friends what happened with the loo paper and laugh about it – but so what? I'd never see any of them again. The only people that mattered were Jules and Tilda, and I knew that no way would they tell anyone, not in a million gazillion years.

When everyone was off the stage, we had to do our routine again and Sarah showed us our positions. She explained how me and Tilda would be on one side of Jess and then Jules would be on the other, and how us three would be a bit back from where Jess was 'cos of her being the main star.

Sarah put some tape on the floor to mark our places and said if we were nervous and suddenly forgot anything we should just smile and watch

each other until we could pick it up again. Just the *idea* that we might forget a bit has made me nervous, but fingers crossed that won't happen. Then we went through the routine again with Sarah standing in for Jess. She said she thought it would be good if Jess did the pointing and wiggling bit with us – how amazing that Jess Moon is actually going to do a bit of our routine!

Then after a couple more practices, Sarah said a big well done and how we had about 2 hours before we were needed again. So we threw our jeans and T-shirts back on and came to this spot on the beach that I agreed with Mum and here I still am! We haven't met Jess Moon yet as she's still on her way back from a TV interview in London apparently (how cool is that!).

Oh hang on, here come Mum, Mr. Van der Zwan and Alex – I am just doing that big wave you do on the beach to demonstrate where you are.

1 hour and 7 minutes later.

The Beach Party has begun!

We have just watched the surf display and it was totally fabulastic! I bet you can guess who was in it with his dad (hee hee!).

Oh, and Mum, Alex and Mr. Van der Zwan are massively happy for us for winning the dance comp! The Beach Party is so amazing – as well as the display stuff, there's a cool food and drinks tent with loads of little cakes that say Hey Girls! on. There is also an area for makeovers and nail painting (though of course we have already done ours!). A DJ is onstage at the moment and lots of people are dancing in front of him, and gathering to get good places to see Jess Moon (and us – yikes!). Plus, there is one of those fairground rides where you sit down in this round thing and get spun

about – oh, I am no good at explaining it. I mean the one that looks like this

We are definitely going on it later!

Right now Jules has gone to play the tombola, 'cos she reckons her luck could still be on full power after winning the dance comp, and Tilda is queuing for the fortune-teller tent to get her future revealed.

Can you believe that in just – hang on while I check my phone – 35 minutes, we are going to be up onstage together, the three BFF, dancing with Jess Moon?

Oh, yeek! Gotta go.

Saturday the 27th of August,

in the car (boo hoo!!!!!).

We are in the people-carrying car going home – it's the first chance I've had to write in here after the whirlwind of excitement that has swept us all up and spun us round. Me, Jules and Tilda are still wearing our shell necklaces to remind us of all the amazingness that has happened.

Mum just said, "Maybe you shouldn't start writing now, Lu, you'll get travel sick." But I have told her there is no danger of that with Mr. Van der Zwan going *soooooo* slowly. I thought she was going to tell me off for a minute, but luckily everyone laughed (even Mr. V). They have finally got that I am being funny and not rude! It's such a relief we don't have to be like the perfect Von Trapp girls after all!

Well, there is so much to tell you I don't know where to start. I will try to say everything in order

and not miss any bits out. The reason I had to suddenly stop writing yesterday was 'cos Jack came up to me!!

I jumped up and dragged him a bit away so Mum couldn't earwig on us, then I realized that I looked too keen and made myself slow down and just, like, *saunter* along next to him towards the waves (it is hard to saunter on sand but I did my best). 'Cos of passing my Surf Language Level 1 (thanks to Tilda!) we could totally talk to each other.

I was like:

Me: You rode your stick without mullering! You rock, grommet!

Jack: Thanks – I thought I was gonna donut, but I nailed that sick wave.

Me: Yeah. You totally did not wipe out.

Jack: Hey, you want to get a drink or something?

I got confused then.

"Sorry, I didn't learn what that one means," I said.

Jack gave me a really weird look and went, "Erm, a drink? You know, liquid that stops you being thirsty? Juice and stuff?"

He just meant a normal drink! And I felt a total idiot again! Except this time I didn't mind, 'cos after the giant **CRINGE** in the dance comp I don't think anything will ever embarrass me again. Besides, you've got to take risks and go for it if you really want something, don't you? So I took a deep breath and said, "That would be rad. I am stoked you asked me."

So I quickly went and told Mum where I was going ('cos I promised to keep her posted at all times, and plus I needed a pound for the drink!). I had to put up with them all going "*ooooooohhhhhh!*" which normally would have been **CRINGE-MANIA**! but like I said, I think I am bulletproof against embarrassment at the moment!

Maybe you only get a certain amount of Cringe Power per week and I'd spent all mine!

Jules and Tilda are reading this over my shoulder even though I have told them the exact words me and Jack said about a million times (we stayed up whispering for ages last night and we had a midnight feast, although it was at about 10.44 o'clock 'cos we couldn't wait till it was actual midnight).

Oh, hang on, Tilda just nudged me and did eyes to mean carry on with the Jack story, so I will.

We walked up the beach together talking in Surf Language and it was really nice. I told him all about winning the dance comp and he was really *stoked* for me and said he'd be watching when we performed with Jess! On the way back we messed around by the waves and when I nearly fell over he grabbed my hand and even when I was safe again and in no danger of getting sea on me he still held on to it – so I knew for sure he liked me then! He only let go when Mum and Mr. Van der Zwan came into view, and we said goodbye till after the concert. How amazingly cool is that?!

But I hardly had time to think about it, 'cos

Tilda and Jules were sitting with the others, waiting for me. It was time to go backstage and get ready for our performance!

Oh, hang on, we are stopping at the services to go to the loo (yes, Mum is saying *loo* now instead of *facilities*, so she must have stopped worrying about being posh in front of Mr. Van der Zwan!).

I'll tell you the rest in a min…

A min later!

When we got backstage, a cool local girl band called Spidergirls were going on, to do a warm-up for Jess Moon.

We were all really nervous and excited as we got our make-up touched up by this nice girl called Lauren. Then Sarah took us to meet Jess and she was so lovely and not at all starry in that way where you want 10 green fruit pastilles to be delivered to your dressing room specially. I got really nervous and started overly talking, like babbling on about her fabuliciousness. And Tilda went bright red and did an actual curtsy like she was meeting the queen! Luckily Jules kept her head and made sensible comments about where we were from and that.

Jess Moon said she loved our costumes, especially the highly original skirts, and she was amazed when I said we made them out of

cagoules. Even just thinking of it now I am **DYING** of chuffedness that she liked my designs. Maybe when I'm a *Real Actual Fashion Designer* she'll want me to create her stage gear for her! Sarah told her about the pointing and wiggling bit and we all went through it together – Jess is so amazing, it only took her about 2 seconds to get it completely right. As we were waiting backstage, we all had a big group hug with her and she went, "Good luck, guys! Go for it!"

Can you believe I have hugged an actual famous pop star?!

So then the DJ, who was also being the presenter-type person, announced Jess Moon and the dance comp winners – Lucy, Jules and Tilda from Sherborne in Dorset (i.e. us!) – and then we were on!

When we walked onstage and got in our places on the floor this big cheer went up for Jess and it was *sooooo* freaky seeing all those people out there looking at us! We laid down on the tape

markers in our beginning positions and I felt so nervous I thought I would have to just stay lying on the floor and concentrate on not throwing up. But when the drummer went *click click click* with his sticks like they do and the song started we just automatically leaped up into our surf positions and began our routine. Soon I forgot all about the people looking at us and we were just having the most amazing time ever. I honestly think we did it the best we ever have. Oh, Tilda and Jules are agreeing!

Afterwards the big cheering and clappingness went on for ages and ages and we had to go to the front and take a bow all holding hands with Jess. Then we had to go off while she did her other songs. But we got to watch from the side of the stage and it was even better than being in the front row of a concert!

That's when I realized that the loo paper cringe had completely faded into the background and vanished away. It is amazing to think that I would

have stopped myself from dancing onstage with Jess Moon and fulfilling my wish, just because of a cringe (a Five Star Cringe, but still!). Yes you have probably guessed it, but now that it has come true I can tell you that for my birthday wish I wished to win the comp – it's so brilliant that we made it happen! I will never ever forget this holiday, even when I'm about 83!

While we were dancing and doing the bow the photographer for Hey Girls! was taking loads of pix, so we are going to be in our fave mag too – how amazing is that?!

It's not out yet (duh, obviously!) so I am going to do a picture of what we looked like. But I'm not going to squash it into this little space, so turn over the page to see how fab we looked.

When it comes out we are all buying about 10 copies each for future posterity. Plus we were given these cool posters of Jess which she signed for us with our actual names on and everything. When she finished she went down the side of the stage and loads of her fans were asking for autographs. Can you believe that some girls were even asking *us* for ours too, 'cos of being onstage with her?! Luckily I have been practising mine for when I am

a famous designer, so it was quite easy to do all scribbly swirly. It's like:

L.J. Hartley

Jules and Tilda want to do theirs too – hang on, I have to pass this journal over.

Tilda Van der Zwan

Julietta Garcia Perez Benedicionatonio

Mum and Mr. VDZ were so proud of us, and for once Alex didn't think I was a yucky older sister but a cool and trendy person who hangs round with famous pop stars – it has lasted

overnight and he is sharing his Rolos with me (of course I ate all mine before we were hardly even in the car).

Oh, but now he is singing, "Lucy loves a surf boy" over and over. I would kick him but I think my new matureness of being a teenager is here at last. Oh whoops, my foot just accidentally slipped and unfortunately caught him on the leg!

Luckily he has helpfully reminded me to tell you what happened with Jack after the concert, though. We met up again on the beach and went for a bit of a walk away from the others, who were all annoyingly going "*Ooooooohhhhhh!!!!*" at me. He said he thought me and Jules and Tilda were rad onstage and also that we rocked. We hugged goodbye and I thought about suggesting we could write to each other. But then I decided not to, 'cos it's nice to just have him as a *Holiday Romance*.

And yes, it *was* a romance, because he *kissed* me! It was in fact *soooooo* romantic with the

waves lapping gently near us and the sun and golden sand (unfortunately there were also about 500 other people there, but never mind). He gave me a cool Surfers Against Sewage wristband to remember him by, too! I am going to wear it at school so I can tell the story of Jack if anyone asks where I got it, which they will because I will wave it in their faces as a hint!

We are nearly home now!

Weirdly, we are all getting excited to be near home, although before the holiday it wasn't interesting at all! This is for all different reasons.

Jules is excited about going home to wait for the phone to ring 'cos she's sure she'll be discovered for her talent after the Beach Party. She says she is missing her family a bit, but mostly she is missing Hombrito, their dog! That is typical Jules. She has her lovely family round her all the time but she hardly even notices them!

I'm straight away going to go round and see Dad, 'cos actually I have really missed him. I can't wait to tell him all about the holiday and especially about meeting Jess Moon. I think I will probably not mention Jack – some things are not for dads to know! This holiday has made me realize how cool Dad really is, by comparing him with

someone else who I will not mention the name of. Tilda is reading this and nudging me 'cos she knows who I mean – whoops! – but she

I love my dad just the way he is, so you can say what you want about him, Lucy Jessica Hartley, and I won't care, so there!

Tilda just wrote that bit, as I'm sure you can guess!

Tilda wants to get home too so that she can go shopping for her new uniform. She says she can't wait to get back to school. Strange. I don't get it, but then, that is the cool thing about people – we are all different.

Oh!

I just sneezed, so Mum asked if I wanted a bit of loo roll from her bag and we all three burst into giggles. She was like, "I just don't understand you girls!" but we weren't going to explain! Hey, maybe I should send a letter about the cringe in to the Hey Girls! Readers' Most Embarrassing

Moments Page. I would most probably win the star prize!

Well, we are nearly down my road now, and I think I will end this journal while we're still on our holiday, kind of, before we step out of the car and back into Normal Life. Plus I am running out of pages! Will write more when school starts!

But till then, lots and lots of summer love from,

Lucy Jessica Hartley

Don't go yet!
My cool quiz is on
the next page...

Lucy Jessica Hartley's Holiday Quiz

What's your top holiday destination? Find out with my fab quiz and then persuade your paries to take you there. Simple, ne c'est pas?

1. Your ideal beach is:

A) Jam packed with interesting people to meet – if you can hardly find space for your towel, you're happy!

B) Miles of empty white sand, with just a coconut tree and a good book for company.

C) A jagged rocky coastline with some really steep cliffs to climb and ginormous waves to surf.

2. Which of the beach eats below would you pick?

3. What do you have in your beach bag?

A) Notebook for swapping addresses with all those fab people you meet on your hols, giant towel to fit all your new friends on.

B) Book, books, nice pamper stuff…oh, and more books!

C) Spare action sandals in case you wear the first pair out, beach ball, frisbee, mini tennis set and first-aid kit.

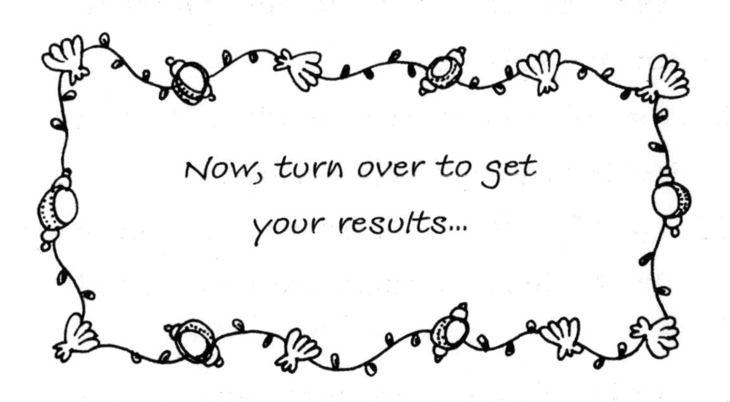

So which one are you?

Mostly As: Beach Queen
To you, a fab holiday is all about people. You love a big crowd and everyone loves you too! Try Florida or sunny Spain for your holiday heaven!

Mostly Bs: Desert Island Babe
For you, holidays are all about the big chill. Try the laidback Caribbean islands for sun-soaked bliss – or go for a spa weekend closer to home!

Mostly Cs: All-Action Heroine
Well, no one will ever catch *you* lazing on a beach! Not when you could be abseiling down things! You'd love to be anywhere where there are waves to surf, cliffs to scale and games to organize – so give Cornwall a try, or even New Zealand!

Totally Secret Info about Kelly McKain

Lives: In a small flat in Chiswick, West London, with a fridge full of chocolate.

Life's ambition: To be a showgirl in Paris 100 years ago. *(Erm, not really possible that one! – Ed.)* Okay, then, to be a writer – so I am actually doing it – yay! And also, to go on a flying trapeze.

Star sign: Capricorn.

Fave colour: Purple.

Fave animal: Monkey.

Ideal pet: A purple monkey.

Worst beach freak-out: Going into a portaloo on the beach and finding a GIANT lizard thing right by my feet – I ran out screaming!

Fave hobbies: Hanging out with my BFF and gorge boyf, watching *Friends*, going to yoga and dance classes, and playing my guitar as badly as Lucy's dad!

Find out more about Kelly at www.kellymckain.co.uk

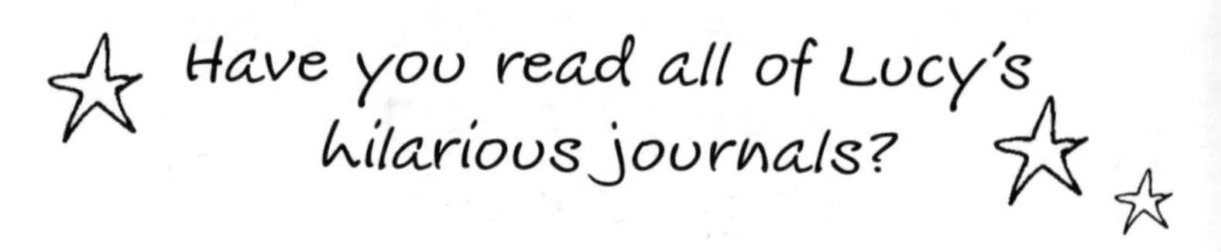

Makeover Magic

Lucy Jessica Hartley is a style queen, so when geeky new girl Matilda-Jane starts at school, she comes up with a fab makeover plan to help her fit in – and learns a few things about friendship, too!

9780746066898 £4.99

Fantasy Fashion

Lucy's fave mag is running a competition to design a fantasy fashion outfit and Lucy is determined to win the fab prize – whatever it takes!

9780746066904 £4.99

Boy Band Blues

Lucy has been asked to style a boy band for a Battle of the Bands competition and she's mega-excited about it – it's just a shame lead singer Wayne is such a big-head!

9780746066911 £4.99

Star Struck

Lucy's won a part as a film extra and decides she must get her fab design skills noticed on screen – but will the director appreciate her original efforts?

9780746070611 £4.99

Picture Perfect

Lucy is in charge of the fashion pages for the school magazine – and she can't wait to get on with the photo shoot! If only she could find a location and some models!

9780746070628 £4.99

Style School

School fashion guru Lucy sets up a style school in the loos, with lessons in accessories, hair and make-up. But what will happen when the School Uniform Police (aka Mr. Cain) finds out?

9780746070635 £4.99

Catwalk Crazy

Lucy is putting on a charity fashion show, but someone seems to be sabotaging all her efforts. Can she track down the culprit and win back her audience before it's too late?

9780746080184 £4.99

Coming soon...

Planet Fashion

Tilda's bedroom is a design disaster, until Lucy and Jules give it a fab, eco-friendly makeover. But could their green project be gorgeous enough to win them a starring role on Tilda's fave TV show, Go Green?

9780746080191 £4.99

For another fab series full of fun,
friendship, secrets and boys,
check out

SUMMER CAMP SECRETS

by Melissa J. Morgan

Miss Manhattan

City chick Natalie is surprised to find that she actually enjoys summer camp – until her big secret gets out...

ISBN 9780746084557

Prankster Queen

Mischievous Jenna is famous for her wild stunts, but this year she's totally out of control. What's bugging her?

ISBN 9780746084564

Best Friends?

Fun-loving Grace starts hanging out with Gaby from rival bunk 3C, before she realizes what a bully Gaby can be.

ISBN 9780746084571

Little Miss Not-So-Perfect

Sporty, reliable Alex seems like the perfect camper. But she's hiding a problem that she can't bear to admit.

ISBN 9780746084588

Blogging Buddies

The girls are back home and keeping in touch through their camp blog. But one bunkmate needs some extra support.

ISBN 9780746084601

Party Time!

Everyone's excited about the camp reunion in New York! But when it gets to party time, will the girls still get on?

ISBN 9780746084618

Three's A Crowd

New camper Tori is from LA and is just as super-hip as Natalie. Good thing Nat isn't the jealous type – or is she?

ISBN 9780746093382

Wish You Weren't Here

Sarah stresses when classmate Abby turns up at camp – will she expose Sarah as a geek to all her fun-loving friends?

ISBN 9780746093399

Just Friends?

Priya's best friend is a boy but she's sure she could never have a crush on him – until he starts to like another girl...

ISBN 9780746093405

Just My Luck

When practical jokes start happening during Colour War, Jenna is the obvious suspect. But could someone else be to blame?

ISBN 9780746093412

Falling in Like

Valerie's wicked stepsister, Tori's forbidden crush, Alyssa's censored artwork...life back home after camp is so complicated!

ISBN 9780746093429

On Thin Ice

Tori's only allowed to invite five friends on her fab holiday weekend. But how can she choose without hurting anyone?

ISBN 9780746093436

All priced at £4.99

Secrets, hopes, dreams...
These girls share more than just a dorm!
Meet the

School Friends

by Ann Bryant

First Term at Silver Spires

Katy is nervous about going to boarding school for the first time, especially as she's got a big secret to hide. The girls in her dorm seem really nice, but when someone sets Katy up for a fall, how will her new friends react?

9780746072240

Drama at Silver Spires

Georgie loves acting and is determined to win her favourite role in the school play. But her audition goes drastically wrong and an older girl steals the show instead. Will Georgie ever get her chance in the limelight now?

9780746072257

Rivalry at Silver Spires

Grace is at Silver Spires on a sports scholarship and feels the pressure to do well in competitions. But when someone starts writing hurtful messages saying she's just a show-off, she loses her nerve. Can she still come out on top?

9780746072264

Princess at Silver Spires

Naomi hates the attention that comes with people knowing that she's a princess. But when she's asked to model in a fashion show, she can't refuse – after all, it's for her favourite charity...what could go wrong?

9780746089576

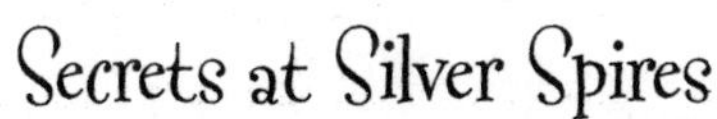

Secrets at Silver Spires

Jess is really struggling with her lessons. She daren't ask her friends for help, because she doesn't want them to find out how stupid she is. But now that she's being made to go to special classes, how long can she keep her secret to herself?

9780746089583

Star of Silver Spires

Mia's ambition is to be a real musician. She'd love to enter a song she's written in the Silver Spires Star contest, but then she'd have to play live onstage too. And performing in public is her biggest fear ever – can she find the courage to overcome it?

9780746089590

All priced at £4.99

For Emily, with love

First published in the UK in 2007 by Usborne Publishing Ltd., Usborne House, 83-85 Saffron Hill, London EC1N 8RT, England. www.usborne.com

Illustrations by Vici Leyhane.

A CIP catalogue record for this book is available from the British Library.

JFM MJJASOND/08
ISBN 9780746080177
Printed in Great Britain.